"I'm coming with you," she said adamantly.

"I'd feel better if you stayed out of sight."

"And let you get hunted down only for them to come find me after they take you out? Not a chance."

Her statement cut like a scalpel to his wounds, affirming his deficits.

"Right. Two is better than one."

He opened the door and took the lead, not wanting to give anyone a chance to take her out without going through him first.

They turned the corner to walk up the steps.

Glass shattered, and Avery screamed as her hand clamped down on Seth's forearm.

Pain ricocheted through his head as an explosion rocked the ground. He twisted and wrapped his arms around Avery's waist and dropped to the ground. Seth shut his eyes, and images flooded his mind. Something wet oozed under his hand. Except he wasn't in Iraq and that sticky substance indicated Avery might be wounded...

Laura Conaway resides in Pennsylvania and creates stories with a healthy dose of suspense and happily-ever-afters. As a former librarian, she's always searching for the next best read and loves solving mysteries like Nancy Drew. When she's not inhaling sweet potato fries to motivate herself to write, Laura spends her time playing guitar and sharing about the Greatest Story written. Laura loves connecting with readers, so visit her website, lauraconawayauthor.com.

Books by Laura Conaway

Love Inspired Suspense

Silencing the Witness

Visit the Author Profile page at LoveInspired.com.

SILENCING THE WITNESS

LAURA CONAWAY

LOVE INSPIRED SUSPENSE
INSPIRATIONAL ROMANCE

LOVE INSPIRED® SUSPENSE
INSPIRATIONAL ROMANCE

ISBN-13: 978-1-335-59935-3

Recycling programs
for this product may
not exist in your area.

Silencing the Witness

For questions and comments about the quality of this book, please contact us
at CustomerService@Harlequin.com.

Love Inspired
22 Adelaide St. West, 41st Floor
Toronto, Ontario M5H 4E3, Canada
www.LoveInspired.com

Printed in U.S.A.

And he said unto me, My grace is sufficient for thee:
for my strength is made perfect in weakness.
Most gladly therefore will I rather glory in my infirmities,
that the power of Christ may rest upon me. Therefore I
take pleasure in infirmities, in reproaches, in necessities,
in persecutions, in distresses for Christ's sake:
for when I am weak, then am I strong.
—*2 Corinthians* 12:9-10

To the One Who writes the best stories and has filled my heart with praise. Soli Deo gloria.

ONE

Avery Sanford couldn't afford to be found alive, or everything she worked for would be destroyed. She needed to lie low this summer until after she testified in the trial against drug ringleader, Antonio Chavez. Her fingernails tapped the school computer keyboard frantically. The students had already left for summer vacation. Avery was one of the last teachers in the building. Only five more exam grades to input, then she'd be a free woman for two months. Well, as free as her current life situation would allow. She was tired of this double life, with the need to protect her identity thanks to the WITSEC program. Although she did the right thing coming forward with proof that could put a criminal behind bars, the consequences of her decision still loomed overhead.

Her stomach rumbled, and she glanced at the time on her computer screen. It was well after six. With no windows in her classroom office to alert her to the outside world, time had escaped her.

She typed in the last student's grade and sat back in her chair with a sigh. Another year as a high school history teacher down. And only four students failed her class. Which meant fewer disgruntled parents who would question their child's grade.

The chair squeaked on the linoleum as she stood and stretched. Time to treat herself to a milkshake and fries from the local burger shack. Drive through, of course. Eagle Point was a small enough town where the high school kids frequented the local establishments, and she didn't want to run in to anyone tonight.

She placed her computer and notebook in her bag and zipped it up. A thud reverberated through the wall on her left, and her hand froze. Her heart skipped a beat as she scanned her office. It had been three years, but she still looked over her shoulder constantly. The fear of them coming to finish their job and follow through on their threat rang in her ears.

Beads of sweat broke out on her palms as she remembered the lethal darts Antonio's murky brown eyes threw her way when he discovered she witnessed him snuff out the life of that helpless woman.

Avery's upper body shivered.

Breathe in. Breathe out.

The repetition helped her mind focus on slow, steady breaths. She'd just wanted to help her friend escape a life of drugs. And it cost Avery a life of normalcy. At least she still had breath in her lungs. But if Antonio and his clan succeeded, it wouldn't be for much longer.

No, she wouldn't let them win. God was with her. There was nothing to be worried about. Yet it didn't eliminate the fear of the unknown and what could happen and the possibility she might need to defend herself.

Enough panic for the day. It was probably the boys' basketball team finishing up their practice. She swung her bag over her shoulder and locked up her classroom.

Her real identity remained hidden from everyone in town, and she, along with the deputy marshals, intended to keep it that way. They would have alerted her to any danger. Still, she couldn't help the gooseflesh that pricked her skin as she headed for the exit. She rounded the corner and slammed into something hard.

A hand grabbed her arm to stop her from falling. A scream escaped her mouth as she wrestled out of the person's grip.

"Whoa. It's okay, just security," a deep, baritone voice said.

Her eyes landed on the one person she'd tried

to forget even existed. Her jaw went slack, and she scrunched her forehead. This man shouldn't be here. Not only because he altered her life in too many ways to count, but her present safety depended on her anonymity among everyone.

The scar along his cheek shone prominently up close and trailed down the side of his neck.

Avery took a step back.

Seth Brown's eyes scanned her from head to toe before he moved to create more distance as well.

"What are you doing here?" Avery bit her tongue to avoid raising her voice.

Seth cocked his head. "Doing a security run." He stated it like she should know the duty of his job based on the silver badge he wore on a ketchup-red shirt.

He might not know who she was anymore, but she would never mistake his face from the photos her brother had of his military buddies. This man was responsible for her brother's death, and seeing him up close was the unpleasant reminder of what she'd lost.

As commander of the platoon, Seth had led Logan straight into an IED and left him to be killed, without saving his teammates. He'd had the means and power to go after the enemy. Instead, her brother ended up on the MIA list until too much time passed and the military presumed him dead.

Avery crossed her arms. "You're not our regular security guy."

"He quit last week. And with the current staff shortage, my boss pulled me in. Although living an hour and a half away isn't ideal," Seth mumbled.

Avery raised her eyebrows. "They can do that?"

"I was promised that it's only temporary." Seth shrugged his shoulders. "I need to go finish my rounds. I heard a noise while locking up and came to investigate. Which way's the gym?"

"Right around the corner." Avery pointed behind her.

Seth glanced down at his watch. "Gotta make sure no kids are fooling around back there when they should have left ten minutes ago."

Fear crawled its way back into the crevices of Avery's mind.

"I see." She repositioned her bag, ready to leave this awkward encounter and get to the safety of her car. "Well, have a good summer."

"Thanks—you too."

She took a few steps toward the exit but stopped at his voice.

"Oh, and congrats on winning the teacher of the year award. From what I've read, the students have a great teacher."

She swiveled on her heel. "How did you know about that?"

"It was in the newspaper on Monday. Gotta love those staff photos they plaster on every announcement."

Nausea worked its way up into Avery's throat. No photos were supposed to be shared of her—ever. Except for the headshot evident on her ID badge that let her into the building. What if she wasn't overreacting about the noise? What if they'd found her and were in the school? She'd feel much better when she was back at the safe house. Behind secure doors.

Despite the sickening feeling in her gut, she kept her tone even. "I've enjoyed working with the kids. They're good most of the time." She smiled. "I'll let you finish locking up. Enjoy your evening."

Not waiting for a response, she made a beeline for the doors, her steps quick and sure. She squinted against the light as she stepped outside. The sun hung low in the sky, shining its rays against her face. But the added warmth provided no comfort. Her car was only one hundred yards away.

Then she'd be safe, where she could look up the article and figure out who to call to take it down.

Up ahead to her right, another car sat parked along the curb. And only one other vehicle occupied the faculty lot where her sedan sat, probably Seth's. But someone loitered at the side of the building.

Footsteps sounded behind her on the pavement as she walked. Each step echoed in time with her pounding heart.

Her hand fumbled in her pocket for her keys, and the cool metal provided comfort as she slipped them between her fingers. If whoever followed behind her tried to attack, she'd be ready. With a black belt in karate, she wouldn't go without a fight. She refused to become a victim.

The footsteps behind her quickened, and she broke into a jog to cross the street, her muscles taut.

"Wait!"

Get a grip, Avery. Paranoia wouldn't be her friend today. They'd already taken too much from her. She refused to let the past win. Her shoulders relaxed at the voice.

She turned around as Seth closed the distance between them, holding a navy bag in his hand. He let out a huff. "Your lunch." He held it up. "Don't want that rotting in the classroom all summer." He laughed and extended his arm.

She took the bag. "Thanks. That would've been an unpleasant welcome-back gift."

"You don't say. You have any plans to celebrate the start of summer?"

Avery wasn't in the mood for chitchat. Especially with this man who'd made mistakes that stripped her of her best friend.

Plus, the added feeling of being watched invaded her senses as the two of them stood alone in the empty parking lot. Exposed. She might as well plaster a bull's-eye on her back.

With a firm click, she hit the remote start button, and her car revved to life. She took a few steps toward the vehicle before a blast of heat and force exploded and propelled her in the air. A scream met her ears, but she couldn't tell if it was her own or not.

Something sharp hit her side before she landed on the pavement. Pain shot through her shoulder, and her head whacked the ground. Black dots danced in her vision as she stared up at the blue sky, the color fading. No, she wouldn't let her life end here. She couldn't die like this, because she still had to see justice served so she could go back to living a normal life. Her mind struggled to stay alert. It sounded like someone called her name, but her mouth couldn't form a response. Without asking for permission, her eyes receded into darkness.

Crouched next to an unconscious woman, checking for a pulse, was not how Seth Brown imagined starting his summer vacation. He had to do something to help her. No one else could die on his watch. But images of the long-ago day in Iraq blipped through his mind, taunting him with déjà vu and the all too familiar reminder of how he'd failed. How weak he truly was. There had been too much blood that day. The smell of death permeated the air, and he could do nothing to stop it. Incapacitated himself, he'd watched the lives of those around him slip away.

"Avery. Can you hear me?" He tapped her shoulder. Her blond hair clung matted to her face, her eyes closed. A cut was evident above her left eyebrow, but the rest of her ivory complexion remained smooth, free of any blemishes.

She moaned in response but didn't open her eyes. Blood trickled at her side. He needed to add compression but didn't want to move her in case she sustained a head injury.

He pulled his cell phone from his back pocket.

"Nine-one-one, where's your emergency?"

"There's been an explosion at Riverton High. In the faculty parking lot off Turner Road. A car's on fire, and a woman's unconscious and bleeding."

"An ambulance and fire truck are on their way. Do you know the woman's name?"

"Avery Sanford."

"Do you know how to apply pressure to Ms. Sanford's wounds?"

"Yes, ma'am. I have medical training and am looking for something to use now."

"Excellent, help is ten minutes out."

He scanned the parking lot. Scraps of debris littered the area. Her car, now a heap of malleable metal, blazed strong. The flames licked up the gasoline. A few feet from the car stood a tree; he hoped it didn't catch on fire, or they'd have an even bigger problem.

The jacket he'd kept in his office as a backup lay next to his bag on the ground. He grabbed it and moved to Avery's right side. A piece of sharp metal was lodged in her side above her hip. He needed to remove it in order to secure the wound and stop the bleeding.

The heat from the blaze breathed down his back.

Images of the convoy rushed through his mind. He'd been in Avery's shoes, lying on the ground, rendered helpless. Except he'd been conscious and aware of the agony on his team's face. On Logan's face.

"Oh, God, not again. Please don't let her die too." The prayer slipped from his lips even though he wasn't confident God would hear his plea. After all, it's not like his previous prayers had changed the outcome for those he cared about. Seth was still plagued with the burden of knowing it was his fault. Now he needed to go it alone to show others he could do a good job.

But what if you kill her too? His mind screamed at him.

Today, that wouldn't happen.

He pulled a pocketknife from his jeans and carefully cut the fabric of her shirt around the wound. The metal was lodged in her skin. Ever so carefully, he removed the piece at an angle, careful not to wiggle it but rather pull it straight out.

Avery's eyes flew open, and she gasped.

The blue in her irises showed torment, like waves buffeting in a storm.

She licked her lips. "What happened?" she asked, her voice hoarse.

"There was an explosion and you fell." He didn't want her to worry about her car right now, so he refrained from mentioning it.

"Explosion?" Confusion clouded her eyes. "My car!" She tried to sit up, propping her good arm under her.

So much for not saying anything. "Whoa, take it easy. You need to lie down. I have to finish tying up your side." He wrapped the jacket around her abdomen then put his hand on her back to guide her back down to the pavement.

"I can't believe this is happening. They must

have found me." She mumbled the words and closed her eyes.

"What do you mean?" He tied the jacket around her waist, pressing firmly to encourage the blood to clot. Her face scrunched in response.

A quick glance at his watch told him the ambulance should be arriving soon. It was a good thing she was conscious now.

"Where's my phone?"

Clearly Avery didn't want to answer his question.

She pushed herself up again, this time rubbing her head. "I need to find my phone."

"Okay. Just rest here. I'll go look for it." He stretched out his hand to keep her from standing.

He stood from his crouched position. Her bag lay several parking spaces down from her car. He jogged over and retrieved it.

"Here you go." He set it down next to her, and she rummaged through the contents. She pulled out papers, a water bottle and some crushed up potato chips. She set her laptop on the ground, a dent bending it upward.

"There it is." She pulled her hand out of the bag. "Oh." Her tone lost its enthusiasm as she inspected the device. A thousand spiderweb cracks covered the screen. She held down the power button, but nothing happened. "It doesn't work." She sat there like a lost child without any sense of direction of where to turn.

"My car." The blaze still surged as flames licked up the gasoline and melted the metal. Tears leaked down her cheeks, and she pressed her hand to her mouth. Her chest heaved.

Seth needed to get her away from the sight in front of her before she went into shock.

"Why don't I help you over to the grass on the curb while we wait for the paramedics?" He extended his hand toward her.

"No. I don't need your help. It would be better if you left. I don't want you tangled up in this mess." Her words tumbled out sharp and punctuated. She pushed herself off the ground using both arms and let out a cry.

The last thing Seth wanted to do was get mixed up in whatever this woman was involved in. But he wasn't coldhearted. He refused to leave her alone without making sure she got the medical attention she needed.

He sighed. "I'm not going to leave you alone in the middle of an empty parking lot when you are injured."

"It's not like you haven't done it before." She mumbled the words under her breath, and Seth had to read her lips to make out what she'd said.

His brow furrowed. What was she referring

to? He didn't know this woman and hadn't engaged in a conversation with her before today. "Look, once the medics arrive, I'll leave. But please let me stay to make sure you're safe until they get here."

"Fine." She pinched her lips together.

He walked next to her as she made her way to the grass, observing her movements to make sure she wouldn't pass out or fall over.

Suddenly, Avery let out a scream and stumbled forward. He grabbed her shoulder to keep her from falling onto the curb, the same moment an object whizzed past her. What in the world?

"Someone's shooting." Panic rose in her voice.

A gray sedan sat near the side entrance of the building with its window rolled down a crack and a gun pointed in their direction.

"In my truck, now," he shouted. He pulled her to the left, willing her to move quickly through the parking lot. Another bullet whizzed past him, and he ducked. The noise of the shots was muffled. If he had to guess, the guy used a suppressor. And thanks to being deaf in his right ear, it made it harder to determine which direction the bullets were going. It seemed impossible for him to get Avery to safety when he couldn't even tell where the danger came from. He pulled open his door and helped Avery in.

"Stay down."

He hopped in the driver's side and put the truck in gear, then peeled out of the parking lot. The backroads near the school didn't normally have lots of traffic, and right now that worked in their favor. He didn't want any bystanders getting mixed up in the cross fire.

He stole a glance at Avery, her face pale as she lay hunched in the seat. At least she'd been able to put her seat belt on.

"I think I deserve an explanation as to what's going on," he said.

The rearview mirror showed the sedan gaining on their tail. A turn appeared up ahead, and Seth swerved around the corner. Unfortunately, the car made the quick move too.

"I don't know what's happening." Hysteria rose in her voice.

"I'd beg to differ." He'd already risked his life for this woman, who resurfaced the memories and PTSD he'd managed to shove aside for years. He wasn't confident they were going to make it out of this situation alive, but she needed to tell him something if they wanted a fighting chance.

"If I had my phone, I would have more details. All I know is my picture should not have been in the newspaper."

"Why—" Seth's words were cut short as he lost control of the truck and it bounced on the road.

"They hit a tire!" Avery shrieked.

"Hang on." He gripped the steering wheel as the truck skidded across the lanes. He eased his foot on the brake, but the truck had too much momentum. Another car approached them in the opposite lane. If he maneuvered left, he'd hit them. But if he turned right, they'd fly through the guardrail and down the embankment. Sweat beaded on his brow as he searched for another way out.

There wasn't one.

With the turn of the wheel, the front bumper slammed into the guardrail. Defeat washed over him as the truck descended the hill. Seth just wanted to make things right and get his life back on track. Not take someone else to an early grave. The reality suffocated him, but there was nothing he could do to stop it.

TWO

Avery's hand gripped the car door handle, the muscles cramped at the intensity of her curled fingers. She wanted to live free of being hunted by the enemy. And rest assured justice had been served. Except she'd failed at the task. Instead, more people were in danger and her parents would have to face the death of another child. To refrain from letting another scream escape, she bit down on her lip and squeezed her eyes shut, prepared for an impact that would surely kill them.

The truck bounced, and she slid in her seat. The vehicle toppled to the left and a thunk met the front bumper and sent Avery's head forward before it whipped back against the headrest. Metal crunched in her ear, and she opened her eyes a sliver at first, before the sight of smoke caused an adrenaline rush.

"Seth!" Her voice came out squeaky. "The truck's on fire."

Seth moaned, and she had to tilt her head to see him below her from her vantage point with the way the truck landed.

"It's just the airbag," he said. A click sounded, and he removed his seat belt. "Can you get yours undone?"

In a swift motion, she moved her arms to feel for the buckle, but the movement caused a flood of pain in her side. She gripped her torso with one hand and used the other to reach for the buckle. "I got it."

"Good. I want you to climb out through the front. Try to avoid the glass if possible."

A wide opening sat where the windshield used to be; jagged pieces of glass jutted from the frame of the truck. On the other side were trees and a sturdy trunk, which must have stopped the car in its tracks. A few leaves covered the mangled gray hood.

"I'll do my best." She used all her upper body strength to push herself up and through. With her feet planted against the back of the seat, she used the surface to her advantage to ease her body out at an angle to prevent any glass from piercing her abdomen.

"I'm out," she hollered back as she slid down the hood of the truck onto the ground. Firm and sturdy. The feeling comforted her.

She was alive. She'd done it. *Thank you, Lord.*

The air around her remained quiet. Eerie. Not a single bird chirped.

Seth grunted.

"Do you need help?" She peered through the window to get a better look. Seth stretched out across the seat. His arms reached for something in the back.

"Give me a sec."

She eased back down to the ground, every part of her body aching. Even her hands trembled.

A disgruntled voice floated through the air.

Avery froze at the sound. Every muscle stiff as if even breathing would alert someone to their presence.

It was impossible to hear what he said from this distance, but she made out a figure at the top of the hill.

Their attacker hadn't left. Avery's heart hammered in her ear, and she wanted to cry but refused to give anyone that satisfaction.

"Seth," she hissed.

"What?" He asked, a little too loudly for her comfort.

"Shh." She spewed the word out in a whisper, and the force of it sent spit flying through the air. "Whoever just tried to kill us is up there. You need to get out of the truck."

"I'm trying."

"What are you looking for?"

"My bag. It must have flown to the back with the descent."

He let out another grunt and tossed a duffel out onto the ground through the windshield.

Avery strained to hear the guy talking, but to no avail. Silence lengthened, then something crunched on the gravel.

If they didn't leave now, she'd be toast. Because this man would finish the job. Sweat erupted on her palms, and Avery frantically turned around, trying to get a sense of her surroundings and which direction to go.

"Are you coming?" Her words sounded lethal as she spoke to Seth. Later she could apologize, if a next time presented itself.

He popped his head out of the windshield. "Yes."

She stood up and peered around the edge of the vehicle up the hill. The dark figure at the top pocketed his cell phone. They had a matter of seconds to make an escape.

"Here." Avery extended her hand up to Seth as he climbed out.

He pushed himself off the hood but froze halfway.

"Would you hurry up already?" Her foot thumped in the grass.

"I can't. My shirt's caught." Seth turned to

look behind him and tugged. "It's snagged on a piece of glass."

Warmth invaded Avery's face. She might die of a heart attack right there. Although it would be better than whatever the person targeting her had in mind.

She reached around to Seth's back and yanked hard on his shirt, but it wouldn't budge.

Shoes crunched on the stones above them.

"Can you just take your shirt off?" Avery asked, panicky.

He raised his eyebrows and gave her a sideways glance.

Right. That's all he had on. He didn't have his jacket anymore, which was tied to her waist, covered in blood.

Think, Avery. Think. You can do this.

She broke off one of the pieces of glass still attached to the windshield. It nicked her palm and a prick of pain slid across her hand. With the shard in one hand and Seth's shirt in the other, she took the glass and cut the fabric away.

"C'mon. Let's go." She dropped the glass in the grass while Seth grabbed the bag.

"That way." He pointed to the right where the trees were thickest. "Follow me."

They ran for several minutes and wove their way around the trees. Avery didn't dare glance back over her shoulder for fear of stumbling or seeing their attacker. By now, adrenaline wore thin, and it hurt to move her muscles. Her lungs burned from all the running.

"Hold on a minute, please." She propped her hand against a tree and bent over to catch her breath.

When her breathing regulated again, she straightened. Seth had stopped, but his stance told her he stayed on high alert, assessing their surroundings.

She couldn't afford to drag this man into the mess of her life. Especially not after all the pain he'd already cost her family. No, she needed to reach a phone and contact the marshals. They were trained professionals capable of helping her.

"You need to leave. Get out of here and go home. I can't have you mixed up in everything."

"I think it might be a little too late for that." His eyes continued to scope out the woods. "And I really don't like us standing here. We're just asking for trouble."

"Fine. Then let's walk and talk," Avery said.

"Bossy much?" He let out a little laugh in an attempt to lighten the mood.

"Sorry. When you're trying to survive, you don't always think before you speak."

Thankfully, Seth seemed content to walk now, because she didn't think her legs would carry her if she had to run.

He moved like he frequented these woods and was in comfortable territory.

"How do you know this area so well?" She looked both ways, unable to gain a sense of direction, even though she'd lived in Eagle Point for several years now. All the talking and moving made her side hurt, and Avery wrapped her arms around her waist. "You said you lived almost two hours away."

"I do. But my brother lives here."

His statement perked up her step. All the more reason for them to diverge paths now.

"Great. Then you keep heading in the direction of his house, and I'll go my way."

"And leave you with an open wound in your side like that?" He pointed to where her arms lay curled. "Not a chance."

His words sent a wave of nausea through her. Like he didn't just abandon Logan to die all those years ago.

"I appreciate the concern, but I will be able to take care of myself. I'd rather you not get both of us killed and make more a mess of the past."

Seth's jaw went slack. What in the world was this woman referring to? Earlier she'd made a similar comment. Did he know Avery from his past?

He tried to think through the events of the last several years and place her but came up empty.

"I don't know what you're talking about, but I'm not a murderer." The conversation escalated the moment the words left his mouth. A stark reality that he clearly hadn't gotten over what he'd done as a soldier.

Memories of when he'd gotten back from Iraq flitted through his mind and reminded him that he should make time to see a counselor. But he'd done a decent job shoving those memories in a dark hole until today.

He should have enjoyed an evening at home, relaxing. And here he stood next to a woman who kept making hostile comments about something intertwined with their past and running from someone who clearly wanted to kill her.

"Are you okay to walk another mile?" Seth slowed his pace until they walked in sync. Her face had paled, and Seth didn't like the look of it. She needed to lie down and rest and have her side tended to.

"I told you I..." She stilled. Her eyes flitted across the grassy area. "Did you hear that?" she asked.

"Hear what?" Now it was his turn to scan.

"Something rustled."

Seth backed up, took hold of her hand and guided them behind the protection of a tree.

If someone hid nearby, it would come down to hand-to-hand combat, because he didn't have his concealed carry with him. There hadn't been enough time to grab it from the glove box before running. And he couldn't keep it on his person now that he worked in a school. He had his eye on a bush several feet away and strained to hear the rustling, even as the leaves shook. Something or someone was there. Seth moved in front of Avery, his legs bent, ready to attack.

The leaves parted and out ran a bunny. He could hear the audible sigh of relief from Avery, and his own muscles relaxed.

"Let's keep moving," he said.

"Fine."

Avery clenched her jaw. Unsure if her quick surrender came from recognizing the danger or because her body was worn out didn't matter. They just needed to get somewhere safe. And his brother's cabin sat beyond the tree line.

For once, he wouldn't joke about Grant needing to live on the outskirts of town in nature and make sure he had enough room for Loki, his beloved K-9 dog.

They continued their walk at a much slower pace, and a limp accentuated Avery's steps. Maybe he should look at her wounds now, given he had everything he needed in the medical bag. But he also wanted to give her privacy. And not risk getting too comfortable out here in the elements with the suspect at large.

"You want to tell me what's going on?"

"I can't."

"You can't? Or you won't?" He didn't mean to sound rude, but this was a serious situation.

"I need to contact someone first so they can tell me what to do before sharing anything with anybody."

"Okay. Fair enough." Thanks to his days in military ops, he understood the need for proper procedures, but the need for secrecy meant whatever was going on was significant.

Avery let out a cough, pain etched in the creases on her forehead.

The sun began its descent and rays of light streamed through the trees and bounced off the ground. It wouldn't last long though. The daylight would evade them shortly.

Clouds dotted the horizon, which meant they wouldn't have much moonlight to navigate their steps. His phone flashlight would have to suffice.

"You don't happen to have any water?" Avery stopped again, her shoulders sagging.

He set down his bag and rummaged through the contents. "Here." He twisted off the cap and handed it to her.

In a few gulps, she'd downed half the bottle before giving it back to him.

"Thanks," she said, wiping her lips with the edge of her shirt sleeve.

Seth took a few sips himself before putting it back in the bag.

"Medical supplies?"

"Yeah. Without looking at it, I can't say for sure, but I'm pretty confident your side is going to need stitches."

The makeshift bandage from the tied jacket held firmly around her waist. "You did a good job wrapping it up though. Thanks."

Her compliment threw him for a loop, and he didn't know how to respond.

"It's what I was trained to do."

"Where did you learn those skills? Considering you're a security officer," she asked.

Was she trying to fish for information from him? Her nonchalant tone made it difficult to tell.

Before speaking, he picked up the bag and started walking again. "In basic training. For the Army."

"I see." She paused, the sound of crickets filling the space. "Those skills must have been put to good use many times."

The words could have knocked him to his knees. Screaming all the ways he'd failed. How he'd been incompetent to save those he'd sworn to protect.

Another cough escaped. This one sounded deeper in her chest than before.

"My brother's house is just around the corner. We're almost there." He spoke the words in an attempt to encourage her to take just a few more steps.

"I… I don't feel good." The words came out rushed and frantic.

He turned to face her, and her body began to sway. She needed to sit down now. Maybe they wouldn't make it to Grant's house.

"Why don't you sit down for a minute?" He stretched out his hand to take hold of her wrist so he could check her pulse, but her body went limp, and she began to crumple.

All his training kicked into high gear, and he swooped in to grab her before she could hit the ground.

He checked her pulse, which remained steady but slow. He set her gently on the ground and repositioned his bag over his shoulder before scooping her back up. Her lean frame deceived him. The woman had muscle, because she weighed more in his arms than he expected.

A few minutes later, he rounded the corner and almost shouted for joy at the sight before him.

The porch lights shone from Grant's house, which meant he was home. As they approached the yard, a bark sounded from inside. Seth carried a moaning Avery up the steps and rapped on the wooden door. He turned around, her limp body still in his arms, and scanned the premises. Nothing set his alarm bells off. But if they'd been followed, they'd be alerted quickly.

In the meantime, he'd take advantage of the space to tend to Avery's wounds then find out who this woman was and how she was connected to his past.

THREE

"Hold still, would ya?" Seth said.

Avery shifted in the chair at the sight of the suture kit. "I really don't think this is necessary." She'd come to her full senses the moment her peripheral caught sight of the thin-tipped sharp scissors he'd laid out on Grant's kitchen table.

Nausea curled in her stomach, and she swallowed. She wished Logan was with her. Even if just to hold her hand and remind her everything would be okay. The brief introduction to Seth's brother when they arrived had widened the gaping hole in her heart at the absence of her own brother that no amount of stitches would fix.

Seth straddled the stool positioned diagonally from her right side. His eyes moved up and down, assessing her. "Well, there is another option if you'd like." He pulled out a large square packet and handed it to her.

"This is a bandage that has a clotting agent.

So it'll stop any further bleeding from the wound."

"Well, you could have offered this sooner." Her words dripped with sarcasm.

"We were a little busy retreating from a shooter." He took the package from her hand. "And there's a catch."

Her eyes narrowed. "Which is?"

"It's only temporary, so you'd still need to go to the hospital to get stitches."

She groaned. "So, there's no way out of it?"

"I'm afraid not." Seth pursed his lips.

Of course. There was no way she had time to go to the hospital. She needed to contact her handler before her attacker relayed information back to his boss, who would send someone to finish the job.

An image of the look in Antonio's eyes as he'd been hauled away in the cruiser before she'd been whisked into the protection agency sent a chill through her body, and she shuddered. That lethal gaze told her he would do whatever it took to pay her back. After three years, she should have been in the clear, but not anymore.

"You okay?" Seth asked.

"Yeah." Avery pulled in a deep breath. "Just get it done and over with."

She unwrapped Seth's jacket from around her

waist and set it on the ground, refusing to look at the wound; otherwise, she'd end up passing out again.

Instead, she focused her gaze on the closed door to the left of the kitchen. Grant had been gracious enough to give them space to get themselves cleaned up, but she'd seen the questions rolling through his mind. They only had a short span of time before he started grilling her and Seth.

"This first part is going to sting a little because I need to clean the area first."

She didn't say anything and averted her eyes.

"But then I have a numbing topical cream, so you shouldn't feel much."

"Mmm-hmm," she said.

"Avery." He said her name gently, yet commanding, and she turned to look at him. A soft smile filled his face. "If you need to squeeze my leg, you can."

She nodded then faced the other direction to avoid seeing any sharp objects. His compassion intrigued her. His demeanor came across gentler. Not the way she'd concocted him to be in her brain.

The wet cloth met her skin at the same moment a sharp sting pierced her side, and she hissed. Her arm flew up, and she grabbed Seth's leg. The soft fabric of his pants provided comfort like a fuzzy blanket.

Several minutes ticked by until Seth said, "All right. That should do it." The stool squeaked against the hardwood floor as he pushed back and stood up.

"That's all?" she asked, surprised.

"Yep." He placed the tools back in the small box and closed it. "There's a bathroom down the hall on your right where you can freshen up." He pointed in the direction. "Grant left fresh clothes in there for you to change into. They were the smallest size he could find when we first got here."

"Thanks." She stood.

Once locked inside the bathroom, she leaned her head against the frame and closed her eyes for a moment to gather her bearings. She really needed to get ahold of Derek Haynes, the deputy marshal assigned to her until after this trial. A date two weeks away that posed more of a threat to make it there alive.

If only she had another burner phone with her, but it was stowed away at her safe house. No matter how nice Grant and Seth seemed, she couldn't use one of their phones to call. It could be traced too easily.

She pushed herself off the wall and grabbed the olive green T-shirt from the counter. It sported a logo for Travis's Car Shop, the local mechanic in town. The fresh laundry detergent fragrance greeted her nostrils, and Avery froze with her arm in one sleeve. It was kind of Seth's brother to give her a change of clothes, but she couldn't accept any more gestures.

She couldn't put her heart on the line like a fish tempted by bait, who would discover its freedom quelled when it was too late to swim away. Avery had been hurt by one too many men who'd suffocated her sense of independence.

Avery lifted up her tattered and bloody button-down shirt. No way could she put this back on.

She held her breath as she slipped into the T-shirt, then scrubbed her hands with the lemon soap.

The sweatpants engulfed her small frame and were baggy, but they would suffice for now. She carefully tied the drawstring then moved her gaze to her side. A white patch covered the area where the stitches were, so she couldn't see anything.

She'd change into more comfortable attire when she got back home.

She walked back out into the kitchen. Seth and Grant stood huddled together talking. At her entrance, Grant stopped and turned. Seth's response was delayed, as if he hadn't heard her approach, but he followed suit.

"Thanks for the clothes," she said softly.

Seth's brother smiled and nodded. "Sorry, that's all I have."

Seth walked over to Avery, his hair wet and spiky. He'd cleaned up too, but the evidence of stubble on his face reminded her of the grueling past couple of hours.

"Avery, I'd like to formally introduce you to my brother, Detective Grant Brown."

Detective.

Oh, boy. He would definitely start asking questions.

She stepped forward and stretched out her hand, and he shook it. "A pleasure to meet you. Thank you for letting us stop by."

"Of course. I'm happy to help. Seth said you've had quite the adventurous few hours."

That was one way to put it.

His brow furrowed.

"Do you have any idea who would be after you? I could run some names in the office."

"That won't be necessary." She pursed her lips. Avery pulled up a kitchen chair and sat down, then regretted the motion as her stitches tugged.

"It won't be a hassle, really. Have you filed a report? I can make sure the ball gets rolling faster." Grant shoved his hands in his front jean pockets.

"I appreciate your offer, but I have capable people already helping me." She crossed her arms in an attempt to get her point across.

Grant narrowed his gaze and observed her. Avery bit the inside of her cheek to keep from squirming under his scrutiny.

"When you change your mind, let me know, and I'll get people on it stat."

Avery gave a polite nod.

Seth opened up a cabinet and took out plates, then went to the fridge. Her stomach grumbled, and she forgot she hadn't eaten since lunch.

"Turkey sandwich?" Seth asked as he plated one and offered it to her.

"Sure." She took it and inhaled a bite. The cold deli meat and juicy tomato satisfied her taste buds.

She finished off the food and stifled a yawn. She couldn't afford to fall asleep now, even though her bedtime approached.

"Thank you for everything, but I should really be going." She stood up and brushed her hands together, letting the crumbs fall onto the plate. She needed to get to her house.

The two men gave each other a knowing look.

"I don't think that's wise," Seth said.

"Why not?"

"It's dark out, and you're injured." He pointed to her side. "I can take you wherever you need to go in the morning."

Avery stood up straighter and carried her plate to the sink. "I really don't want to inconvenience you. Or put anyone else in jeopardy."

"Trust me, it's not a problem. I don't want to be tangled up in this any more than you. But you need rest, and tomorrow I'll drop you off where you need to go, then I'll be out of your hair."

She peered out the window. Darkness crouched at the door and made visibility harder. "All right," she said.

Every hour, Avery glanced at the red numbers on the clock in the dark room. A continual reminder of the sleep she wasn't getting. She tossed and turned in the guest room she'd been given, unable to find a comfortable position for her side while also itching to get a move on. The longer she stayed here, the more risk of someone finding where she'd run off to. And she would never forgive herself if anything happened to Seth or Grant.

She remembered the notes. The thick black ink scrawled on the paper. A warning that they would finish the job with her and everyone she cared about. Antonio had been aware of the cruel punishment she'd endure to see others hurt on her account. Avery pinched her eyes shut. She wouldn't give them the satisfaction. Which meant she needed to do it alone.

With a grunt, she gingerly rolled over to her good side and peered at the clock once more.

Five thirty in the morning. She strained her ears to listen for any sign of someone being up, and when she didn't hear anything, she eased out of bed.

She'd make her way back to the edge of the road and follow it until she got back to her house. The likelihood of the shooter still being at the wreck was slim, considering police had probably investigated it if someone called it in. She gulped. No use chickening out now.

She grabbed her purse and a flashlight from the nightstand.

As quietly as possible, she tiptoed into the kitchen and found a pen and paper to write a short thank-you, then slipped out the front door.

The edge of daylight peeked through the sky as she made her way back through the woods, hoping she remembered how they came. Birds called out in the early morning, and with each step, her heart pounded in anticipation of someone hiding in the fading shadows.

The whiz of a car echoed in her ear. With a few more steps, she entered the clearing, and the familiar scene they'd left behind greeted them.

Footsteps shuffled nearby, and Avery froze.

Had someone followed her? If it was Seth, wouldn't he have alerted her to his presence by now?

She inched up against a tree to listen. When nothing else caught her attention, she took a step forward, but a hand grabbed hers and yanked her back. Before she had a chance to let out a scream, the other hand clamped down over her mouth. She'd been foolish to head back by herself. Avery's stomach coiled. She'd walked right into a killer's snare, and no one would find her.

Seth shot up in bed and ripped the covers off. Perspiration ran down his brow. It took a moment for his eyes to adjust to the darkness, but he made out the dresser on the opposite wall. With a sigh of relief, he swung his legs over the edge of the bed.

He was in Grant's house. Not Iraq. The nightmare and vivid scenes still clung to the recesses of his mind in an attempt to draw him back into a restless sleep with those horrid memories.

It had been several years since he'd succumbed to night terrors, but the events of the last few hours made them seem real once more.

He slid his feet into a pair of socks and padded across the floor, mindful to open the door quietly. A glance back at the clock told him it was only six, and he didn't want to wake Avery. She needed the rest.

He opened the door without a sound. So, Grant finally put some WD-40 on the hinges. He passed the guest room where Avery slept and noted the closed door. No light shone through the bottom crack. Hopefully she slept better than he had.

With the press of a button, Seth flicked the microwave light on and filled a glass with water from the fridge. The cold liquid sent chills coursing through his body and washed away the remainder of the heat that enveloped him.

His stomach grumbled. Time to scramble up some eggs and bacon. A clink echoed as he set his glass on the counter, and he winced. The noise sounded much too loud in the quiet space. He turned to grab a banana from the bowl of fruit, and a piece of paper sat propped against it.

He carried it over to the light, and what he read made his heart stop. In a few short strides, Seth closed the gap to the guest room and knocked.

"Good morning. Avery?" he whispered.

When she didn't respond, he wiggled the knob. It was unlocked, so he opened the door and found the space unoccupied and immaculate. No trace of anyone being there.

Avery had left.

At some point between them turning in for the night and now, she'd snuck out.

Seth swiveled on his heel and came face-to-face with his reflection in the mirror. The indent from the scar on his cheek was rough as he trailed his thumb down the length of it.

Clearly it wouldn't be wise for him to get involved after the flood of dreams. And Avery had decided to leave him high and dry just like his fiancée after his discharge from the Army. His discharge might have been an honorable one, but all his fiancée had seen were his injuries. She'd gone off to find someone better and left him in the dust.

If he went after Avery, Seth's heart would only get hurt with more reminders of his broken past.

He'd already promised to be out of Avery's hair once she'd made it back to her house safely. Could Seth really say he'd held up his end of the bargain if he couldn't confirm she'd gotten home? But he also couldn't stop her from ducking out unprotected. He could go about his life like yesterday never existed.

The grandfather clock struck the hour. Each chime reverberated in his chest as he paced the length of the hallway. There was no way to even know where she'd gone. Because the note told him to stay away and out of her mess.

His brain ran a mile a minute. He couldn't stand around and twiddle his thumbs.

His stomach growled, and Seth walked back to the stove and pulled out a frying pan. He ignited the gas.

What do we always do? Leave no man behind! The command he gave his platoon during training echoed in his mind.

Seth drooped his head. He needed to fight if he wanted to redeem his failures.

He flicked off the burner and grabbed a sweatshirt before heading out to the garage. He quickly doubled back to grab a gun from Grant's safe. The early morning air nipped at his exposed face, and the sun started to make its presence known.

With a quick text to Grant to let him know he needed to borrow the motorcycle and had taken a gun to go investigate the crash and call a tow truck, he hopped on the bike and twisted the throttle.

The engine revved to life, and he meandered his way down the winding back roads. Seth was shocked to see his vehicle up ahead after five minutes. Walking through the woods injured had added a lot of extra time to the escape.

He eased the bike up next to the guardrail. Well, where it used to be. The metal bent and twisted where the truck went over. In the daylight, the vehicle appeared mangled, even from the distance at the top of the hill. No wonder the attacker had been confident he'd killed them.

With the wheels upturned and the front hood bent inward, it was a nasty sight. Even the headlight dangled by a thread.

Seth stepped over the guardrail and surveyed the descent down. Movement to his right caught his attention. He shifted his stance to get a better view and expected to see a deer grazing on the early morning dew-covered grass.

Instead, two people stood in the field. The woman's strawberry blond hair swung around in a ponytail, and the other person secured a tight grasp on her waist. No other cars occupied the road. What were these two doing out here so early?

Suddenly, the woman's hand writhed free from the embrace to swing through the air. Her palm connected with what must be the other person's face as a scream echoed, and a few choice words followed.

Several birds took flight from their perch on the trees.

Seth bounded down the hill. "Hey!" he yelled. Both people moved, and Seth got a better look at their faces. "Avery!"

The man had come back to finish his job. And he was succeeding. He'd grabbed Avery's arms, wrapped them around her side and began to drag her.

In a moment, Seth drew his gun and pointed it at the ground. If an opening presented itself, where he had a good shot of the man without the risk of the bullet striking Avery, he'd take it. Regardless of her impression of him and insisting he not intervene, he wasn't about to let her get kidnapped.

Rocks and pebbles lined the embankment. But he couldn't take his eyes off Avery. If her kidnapper got her deep enough into the trees, he'd never forgive himself.

"I'd advise you to let her go," Seth cupped his hands and said, only a few yards from them now.

No one fired back a response. Avery's eyes widened, even as she pinched her lips.

The guy sported a ski mask and held her firm against him. At least she faced Seth. He needed to come up with a plan and somehow communicate it to her.

The knife's blade caught a glint off the sun's rays, which now made its full appearance and beckoned the start of a new day.

One that unfortunately seemed too similar to yesterday.

With a flick of the wrist, that knife could do serious damage. Although maybe the attacker didn't want her dead anymore. It seemed impossible to decipher what sick game he played.

Seth took a step closer.

Avery squirmed in the man's grasp, but the movement cost her as the knife swiped against her forearm. A whimper escaped her lips.

"Don't come any closer." The man spoke in a gruff voice.

"What do you want?" Seth asked, playing dumb. If he could get the guy talking, the distraction could work in their favor.

"Her," he said. A wicked smile curled on his lips and lifted the edges of the black fabric of the mask.

Avery looked Seth dead in the eyes, willing him to read her mind. "Not today," she said, and lifted her leg and swept it around the man, who stood stunned. With a shove, he fell to the ground.

Seth ran toward her and grabbed her hand to pull her to safety, but her body jerked backward, and she screamed, trying to loosen her foot from the man's grasp.

Seth lifted the gun and took aim.

He had let evil men take too many of his buddies because of war before. Today would be different. Seth needed to protect the innocent. Prove he could do something good. And it started with getting Avery out of this alive.

FOUR

The man's iron grip on her ankle loosened, and with all her might, Avery kicked her leg and began to run. Her ears rang incessantly from the gunshot and made it hard to hear, but she didn't dare look behind her for fear of what would cloud her vision. Seth had come to her rescue. Although she'd have preferred neutralizing the situation herself so that no one else got hurt, she was thankful to still be alive.

Avery kept her fingers intertwined in Seth's as they climbed up the hill, not wanting to let go for fear of being back in her attacker's grasp. They moved at a much slower pace, the ascent steep, and her muscles ached.

She tugged on his arm, indicating they should pause for a minute. The ringing had subsided, but everything still sounded muffled, her own voice foreign.

Seth shook his head and started walking again, this time backward so his gaze remained on hers. "He's not dead—we need to keep moving."

It took her a moment to register what he said as his lips formed the words. With understanding, her eyes widened, and she quickened her pace.

Her attacker made his way toward the hill, one hand clutched to his thigh. Blood oozed down the side.

"Where do we go?" Avery asked, using every ounce of strength to push forward. But her calf muscles screamed in protest at the exertion. Her body hadn't been this sore since she'd first started karate classes when her classmates and instructor pushed her beyond her physical limit at the time.

"I have Grant's bike up there," Seth turned and said. "You can do it."

He was right. This moment called for mental strength. She needed to persevere and tell her mind she could do it. It was truly amazing what the body was capable of doing when you didn't give in. It could endure much more physical stress than most realized.

And if she wanted to live, she needed to hustle. The realization sent a course of adrenaline that rushed through her veins, and she began to jog, matching Seth's pace.

He turned and offered her a smile of encouragement.

Her shoes hit the pavement, and she wanted to shout for joy. Safety lay only a few feet away.

In a moment of confidence, she turned, expecting to see the area around them void of anyone else. Instead, a black ski mask appeared over the side of the hill. The knife blade flashed as the man stood up.

"Run!" Avery yelled. The reflection blinded her for a minute, and she blinked.

Avery stumbled across the pavement as her eyes regained focus. She barely climbed on the motorcycle before Seth sped away and moved in a zigzag motion to make them a harder target.

Her eyes drilled into the rearview mirror, anticipating an entourage of vehicles pursuing them. But they were the only ones on the road.

"Where are we going?" Seth asked.

She assumed he wanted directions to the safe house. "When you get to Elm Road in a mile, make a right." Her arms clung to Seth's forearms, and her head rested close to his face as she spoke.

Warmth invaded her cheeks, and it had nothing to do with the wind whipping against her skin. Easing back as much as possible without feeling like she would fall off the speeding bike, she created distance between them.

She would not become dependent on this man. Not after the mistakes he'd already made.

Her brother had trusted Seth with his life in Iraq, and it had earned him an early grave. She didn't want to risk making the same mistake. Just because her life was in jeopardy didn't mean she needed his help.

They pulled up to her house, and Avery was thankful she hadn't seen anyone else follow them. She eased off the bike. The movement pulled at her side, and she winced.

"Thanks for the ride. I've got it from here." Avery slid her hands into her leather jacket.

"That's it?" Seth climbed off the bike. "No 'Thanks for saving me from an attempted kidnapping or stabbing'?" Annoyance danced in his words.

His eyes searched hers, and she softened her shoulders. "I'm sorry. I'm not thinking straight." She rubbed the palms of her hands against her eyes.

"Hey, it's okay." Seth rounded the bike to close the distance, the helmet in the crook of his arm.

"I'm just scared and don't want people getting hurt." Avery sighed.

"That's understandable considering the circumstances. Do you want to talk about it?" Seth's eyes scanned the perimeter of the front yard.

"No. You did your duty and dropped me off

at my house." Avery walked up the front steps and opened the door, then turned around ready to wave goodbye and nearly fell right into his chest.

"At least let me make sure there's no one lurking in there. After all that's happened, who knows what stunts those people are willing to pull." Seth took a step forward, but Avery blocked the entryway.

"I'll go clear the house. You can keep watch out here. Make sure no one approaches." Derek, the deputy marshal assigned to her case, stood on the other side of the door, so she was safe. And if she stalled long enough, Seth might get antsy and leave.

Before giving him an opportunity to respond, she shut the door and flicked on the entryway light. Despite the sun now shining through the clouds, with her curtains drawn, everything seemed dark.

But it shouldn't be.

After all, this was a safe house. Quite literally a place the marshals had full confidence would protect her, where she could live a somewhat normal life until after the trial.

Derek paced in the living room. His back remained to her, and he ran his fingers through his hair. "What do you mean?" he barked.

Avery cleared her throat.

Derek spun around, his eyes wide. "Where have you been?"

"They found me." Tears gathered in her eyes.

"I know. And you weren't answering your phone. Where is it?"

"Destroyed," Avery hiccupped.

Avery went into a speedy explanation of everything that happened within the last twenty-four hours and how she suspected the picture in the newspaper tipped Antonio's crew off.

Derek grabbed his laptop and typed away. "I'm getting someone to investigate your leaked picture and take it down immediately."

"Thanks. I'm assuming it's been quiet here?"

"Nothing out of the ordinary. But we need to get you relocated stat."

Avery wanted to curl up in a ball and forget everything. Nothing in her life would ever stay normal.

"What about my parents?" Avery plopped down on the couch. Her dad used to work for the police department and started an investigation into the cartel. He'd built evidence with the help of his partner and even put some of the men lower on the totem pole away. When she witnessed the murder, her dad resigned from the force due to a conflict of interest. A lot of people on both sides of the law knew his involvement on the police force and his relation to Avery before he went into WITSEC with Avery's mom.

"All good on the home front." He held up his phone. "I just got off a call with their deputy marshal."

She was glad to hear that. Her parents lived several hours away, and it had been too long since she'd seen them. They'd been offered to go into the program together, but Avery didn't want to put them in jeopardy. Let alone make it easier for Antonio's men to take them all out.

"I'm going to get settled." Avery stood up. To put her mind at ease, she turned on every hallway light and surveyed each room, checked the closets, looked behind doors and even peaked under her bed—a practice she'd only had as a child.

Except now, someone prepared to pounce on her and exact revenge.

She knelt down on her bedroom carpet and twisted the dial of her safe. The lock clicked in response to the correct combination, and she grabbed another burner phone from a pile.

Avery walked over to her window and lifted the curtain away to see that Seth still stood in her driveway, talking to someone on the phone. She supposed she had her dad, who was a cop, to thank for her streak of independence as well.

Satisfied with her search of the house, she

made her way back to Derek. "There's one more thing." Her conscience debated whether to say anything at all, but she couldn't lie.

"Seth Brown, a new security guard from Riverton High, is outside. He was there when my car exploded and made sure we escaped." There was a strong probability they'd want to put him in protective custody as well now that he'd been seen with her or make sure he didn't pose a threat. And considering the reach Antonio had, even from his prison cell, no one was safe.

"I see." Derek chewed on a pen cap. "We're going to keep him close by. I'll run a background check now and make sure he pans out all right."

"But…" Avery didn't know what to say. They were supposed to tell her to make sure he stayed far away from her and found a place of safety for himself. Not with her. "I don't…" Avery let her words trail off.

"No buts. He's part of the case now."

Avery paced the length of the hall and tried to think of a convincing argument.

A pounding resounded on her door. Her heart skipped a beat, and she put a hand over her chest to calm herself. Derek took long strides toward the peephole, and Avery hoped Seth only stood on the other side because she hadn't reappeared yet.

The loud knocking persisted, and Avery stood frozen as the doorknob jiggled.

Someone could have hidden in Avery's house and attacked her. Seth had finished his phone call to Grant to make sure he filed a report for the shooting and sent officers to the scene to investigate. The department excelled at thoroughly assessing a scene to locate evidence. He had relayed as much information without knowing all the details of the situation.

It had been ten minutes since Avery had shut the door in his face. The nerves in his spine tingled. He continued his pounding on the door. When he tried the knob, it resisted. Of course, she'd locked it. Seth pulled his fist back, prepared to bust down the door, when it swung wide open.

A man stood tall in the doorway, and Seth took a step back, shocked to see someone else answer. He hadn't seen anyone sneak around the perimeter.

He narrowed his eyes. "Who are you? Where's Avery?" His hand moved to his holster.

"It's okay. I'm here, Seth." Avery's voice came from inside and the man moved to the side for him to get a better view. A look of relief washed over her face before a scowl creased her forehead.

"I presume you're Seth Brown?" the man asked.

"Yes, sir." He gave the guy another look over and figured he must be well over six feet, because Seth had to arch his head back to meet his gaze.

"And you are?" Seth inquired.

"Deputy Marshal Derek Haynes."

"Get in here. Please." Avery motioned with her hand for him to hurry up. Seth eased past Derek, who stretched his neck out the door to survey the front yard.

"What took you so long? I thought someone found you," Seth said, irritated. He assessed the expanse of the area and walked toward the living room before collapsing on the couch. He propped his leg up on the cushions.

"I had to fill Derek in," Avery said as she sat down on the sofa adjacent to him.

"What did he say?" he asked. The look of disgust on her face told him she wasn't happy about whatever it was. And he still didn't know why she despised him. This woman was feisty and independent, and she had secrets he was clearly unaware of. Would she finally give him some insight? A deputy marshal posted at her house meant serious business.

"You're considered part of the case now. The marshals want you close by."

"What?" The word came out firm, and Seth grimaced. He shouldn't have responded like that. "I'm sorry. I shouldn't have raised my voice."

"Thanks." Avery offered him a small smile. "Although you were the one who wanted to make sure I stayed safe."

Her eyes focused on his, studying him.

"Of course, I wanted to make sure you were safe. But I don't want to be part of this—" he shrugged his shoulders "—whatever situation this is. It's already resurfaced enough haunting memories from my past." Had he voiced that last part in his mind? Obviously not, given Avery's hard-set jaw.

"From the military," she whispered.

How did she— Seth didn't remember mentioning anything about his time serving his country in the past few hours.

"How do you know about that?" he asked and narrowed his eyes.

A knock at the door jolted them both from their seats, and Seth drew his weapon, but Derek beat him to the front entrance.

His heart thudded in his ears with anticipation at who might be on the other side.

Derek turned back to Avery. "Get down behind the couch. Just in case."

She complied, and Seth made his way to the

door to cover Derek. Somehow, he'd gotten himself roped into defending a woman who he didn't remember but who clearly knew him. A job he didn't sign up for, yet he wouldn't be getting out of it anytime soon.

Derek stepped up to the peephole and peered out, then moved the curtain from the side window to get a better look.

"There's a man with a dog. Are you expecting someone?"

"That's my brother," Seth said.

Derek didn't even acknowledge his presence and focused on Avery instead.

"I can confirm that," she said. "I met them last night. He's a detective."

Derek opened the door, and Grant stood with Loki, who barked in excitement when she saw Seth.

He gave Loki a rub on her head and scratched her favorite spot just behind her ears.

Avery walked over to meet them and shook Grant's hand. They exchanged pleasantries before she turned her back toward him and lasered her gaze at Seth.

"You called your brother?" she said in a whisper that came out strained.

He ignored her comment and walked back over to the couch.

"Grant had some officers comb the scene

over on Turners Edge to see if they could find anything on the culprit," Seth said.

"Whoever it was disappeared well before my guys arrived," Grant said, "but it was worth a shot."

"I figured he could help us quicker and pull a few strings if you have anything to add," Seth said to Avery.

"Were they successful in finding anything?" Derek pulled out his phone, fingers poised to start typing.

"We picked up some footprints and a few drops of blood. Forensics will have more in a few days."

Derek finished jotting down notes and pocketed his phone. "Thank you." He shook Grant's hand. "Please let me know when the results come in. Anything is better than nothing."

"Certainly. You'll be the first to know." Grant nodded.

Seth wanted reinforcements if he'd been roped into this. A man never went out to complete a mission alone. There were always buddies covering your back. Yet the risks involved for the men remained evident. One wrong step could get them all killed.

And he was glad Grant had his back. To see him step in and help a stranger showed his character too. One Seth sought to live up to every day.

"If there's nothing else you need here, Loki and I must head back to the station," Grant said as he tugged on his dog's leash. "I'll let you know if I hear anything." He smiled at Derek once more. "Nice to meet you."

All three men stepped onto the porch.

A car sat parked at the end of the drive along the curb, and Seth's muscles tightened.

"Did you bring anyone else with you?" he asked his brother.

"Just the girl and I," he said and rubbed Loki's back.

"Then who's that?" Seth motioned with his head toward the vehicle to be discreet and turned to Derek.

"Are you expecting any visitors, Avery?" Derek turned to face Avery still in the open doorway.

"No. Why?" She drew out the words with skepticism, like she wanted to know the answer.

"Then I'd say you have an unwelcome guest who just arrived," Seth said. Someone determined to get to Avery. It made Seth sick to his stomach. "There's a car parked at the end of your drive."

Avery moved to the window and slid the curtain back ever so slightly to get a glimpse.

Whoever was there though would be outnumbered.

"Head to the basement, now." Derek positioned his form in front of the doorway.

Avery nodded.

"I'll go with her," Seth said.

"Nuh-uh. Not so fast." Derek held up a hand. Several seconds ticked by as he scrolled through his phone, his lips pursed. After what seemed like eons, Derek nodded, content with his findings. "You're clean."

It didn't surprise Seth he'd come back in the clear. But those were precious moments someone could have used to make it up the driveway.

"You'll know it's me giving you the all clear, because I'll call. Got it?" Derek waited for Avery to acknowledge the plan.

"Ten four," she said.

"I'll join you outside," Grant said. "Let's figure out what this person wants." He unhooked Loki's leash.

Seth opened his mouth to protest, but Grant gave him the "now's not the time to argue" look.

Avery led him to the basement, and Seth wanted to pray for their protection as Grant and Loki headed out the front entrance. But he wasn't sure what difference it would make. After all, when it'd mattered most, it hadn't impacted anyone for the better. The door closed behind him, and they made their way into the dimly lit area.

If he called his brother to help only to lead him into a trap that got him injured, it would be one more reason to add to the list of all the ways he'd failed people and solidify the truth that his weaknesses hindered his ability to help.

"What are you waiting for?" Avery waved him over. "This way."

A low growling bark echoed through the closed door, and Seth stilled. He tensed his calf muscles ready to bolt back up the stairs. More inaudible voices rose, and Seth clenched his fist.

He had two people to protect, but he couldn't be in more than one place. So who would it be?

FIVE

Avery squared her shoulders and held her head high. She refused to let Antonio terrorize her. It should have registered in her mind that they'd try to silence her with the trial so close. But she would be a big girl and make sure they didn't succeed. Even if she had to do it herself. But everything had been fine until the picture of her surfaced.

Seth still stood at the top of the stairs.

"You can go out with them if you want." Avery shrugged her shoulders. Loki's bark had made her jump, and Avery could only imagine the confrontation happening outside these four walls.

Seth shook his head and headed in her direction down the basement steps. "They've got it under control. I'd only be an interference now. And I don't want to leave you alone."

Avery nodded. How had it come to this point

where she needed a constant security detail?
More people who put their lives at risk for her.

"You okay?" Seth asked like he could read
her mind. Or maybe he'd heard her grind her
teeth.

She turned to face him. "Peachy. They're not
going to win."

A knowing look crossed his face that she'd
avoided directly answering his question. "I have
no doubt about it." He surveyed the expanse of
her basement, most of which remained unfin-
ished except for one room. "You want to tell me
who 'they' are?" he asked.

Avery pondered his question. He'd already
done a lot to make sure she hadn't died, and
Derek had been adamant about Seth being part
of the case now. "I suppose I owe you an explanation," she said.

"And I would greatly appreciate it."

"Let's go over here." Avery pointed to the finished room that housed all her workout equipment. When she'd arrived here three years ago,
Derek had been kind enough to make sure she
had a space to exercise. And the doors to the
room were lined with tinted windows. So when
she got into a mode, no one could startle her,
because she'd see them coming first.

When the marshals had been confident no im-
mediate threat existed, she'd been allowed to live

here by herself. But the last six months before the trial, they amped up security again. Avery's stomach curled. Clearly, it had been needed.

She closed the door behind them, and Seth let out a whistle.

"Girls can work out too, you know." She raised an eyebrow.

He held up his hands. "I wasn't indicating that at all. I was more impressed with the array of equipment you have."

This man came chock-full of unexpected comments. "Well, in that case, thank you."

He glided his hand over the rack of weights she had in the corner then eased himself onto the bench press and straddled it. His biceps accentuated as he braced his arms alongside the seat.

He was definitely not bad to look at. All those years training in the Army had paid off. What in the world was she thinking? This man was a reminder of all she had lost. Considering the fine lines that creased his forehead, and the scar down the side of his cheek, he still carried the weight of it all. Perhaps the assumptions she had about him were incorrect.

"Who is finding every possible avenue to silence you?" Seth's words pulled her from her trance.

Avery leaned against the wall to keep her side

as straight as possible. This vantage point gave her a view of the basement steps and Seth. She slid off her jacket and draped it over her arm. "It's a long story."

Seth glanced at his watch. "We've got time." He smirked, and a dimple protruded.

"I witnessed a drug deal gone wrong, and someone was murdered." She let out a sigh. The memories flooded back into her mind from that night.

"Hence the marshals involvement."

"Yes. I could easily identify each person there."

"So, how did you get mixed up in all this?"

Avery grimaced. Seth probably didn't mean it to sound accusatory, but it stung to remember how her idea of helping her friend affected her life.

"I volunteered with my church's addiction recovery program. I minored in psychology in school, so I taught some of the classes and helped people get back on their feet. I became a close friend and mentor to a woman named Chelsea who expressed a desire to end the relationship she had with her drug dealer boyfriend."

"Okay," Seth said, and nodded, trying to follow all the pieces she was explaining.

"So I told her I'd go with her for moral support when she ended things with him. Except when we got there, Dominic's cousin Antonio was there, and they were in the middle of a drug deal. I stayed in the shadows at first and called 911. But things got aggressive with the woman who'd come to get her drugs, and Antonio wasn't happy with the compensation, so he shot her."

"What happened when the cops arrived?" Seth asked, pacing the length of the room now.

"When Chelsea saw what happened, she screamed and ran toward the shrubbery at the corner of the house where the men stood. Without thinking, I went after her and—" she shuddered "—thankfully the cops pulled up then. Dominic made a run for it, but Antonio is serving time. Chelsea was taken into protective custody as a witness too, but we haven't had contact since then."

"Wow. So you think Antonio is the one calling the shots?"

"Absolutely. When he saw me that night, words of hate spewed from his lips. And when the man attacked me early this morning, he told me he was ready to finish the boss's orders." Bile rose in her throat as Avery spoke the words out loud.

"And thus far he hasn't succeeded."

"Exactly."

"How have you gotten through all this?" Seth

rubbed his temples, either from exhaustion himself or from grasping the turn of events in Avery's life.

"God's grace alone."

"And that's been enough for you?"

"When I didn't have anyone else, it had to be. There was no ability to contact anyone, so I began to savor the time I had with God. Studying the Bible. It's fascinating to read the story of redemption from beginning to end. He really is the best friend and companion."

"Even when He allowed all this to happen?" Seth asked.

"Well, I mean, He is God, isn't He?"

"I suppose so. It's hard to grasp though, when awful things happen. If God is good, why would he allow that girl to die, or…" His words trailed off, and he hung his head.

The sorrow that filled his expression knocked the breath from her, because the words he refrained from saying spoke volumes. The torment he still lived with after the atrocity in Iraq. Maybe she should just ask him about his time abroad.

Seth looked back up at her as if willing her to say something, anything to fill the silence.

"I get it. Hence, part of the reason I kept up with karate and set up this area." Avery swept her hand across the room. "It's helped me stay sane and feel like I have a part to play in making sure I'm on guard and prepared for anything." It also gave her a taste of home. A special bond she had shared with her dad as a child.

A thud sounded outside, and Avery froze. "What was that?"

Seth stood up and stretched his legs. "What was what?"

"That thud. You didn't hear it?" That was the second time he hadn't picked up on sounds. Had the gun going off the other day caused hearing loss?

He gave her a quizzical look before pulling out his phone. He shook his head. "Grant hasn't texted. Did Derek call?"

"No new notifications," Avery said and waved her phone.

Seth glanced between her and the door, debating what to do. "Let's give him a few more minutes, then I'll go check on him."

Avery folded her arms across her chest and nodded. She was being paranoid. Maybe it had been nothing, and she had imagined something. Besides, Derek was a pro. And Grant seemed like a capable detective. Plus, they had Loki.

Avery took him by surprise. How could she so confidently answer that God remained good even in the midst of tragedy?

Seth couldn't fathom how He'd let half of his platoon die in Iraq. At one time, he wanted to do great things for the Lord. Protect his country and see justice served. And he'd been repaid with battle scars both inside and out. Including the deafness in his right ear. Which he should tell Avery about if they were going to be up front and honest about things.

"I wish I had the kind of confidence you had," he said.

"In?"

"In God."

"It takes time…and trust," she said, her tone kind.

"At one point I did. And then everything spiraled out of control, and I was left with nothing."

"Hence the scars on your face." She cocked her head, not in a judgmental way but rather trying to understand.

Out of habit, he trailed his finger down the side of his face. The place where the shrapnel had once been embedded in his flesh. "Yeah. And the loss of hearing in my one ear."

"Oh, wow. I didn't realize."

"Normally it's not a problem, and I'm able to cope by reading people's lips or turning my good side toward them."

"But other times you're startled, like after I freshened up at Grant's house."

"Exactly."

She opened her mouth then closed it, waiting some time before saying, "You want to talk about it?"

Did he? Not really. The resurrection of the memories and speaking them out loud would only bring terrors when night fell. Avery still stood with her back against the wall, prepared to move if the need arose. A fighter stance he recognized and had taken on frequently himself during his tour in Iraq.

She had the right mindset and capability to defend herself. Her toned physique and eagle eyes told him as much. So then why was he here? It's not like he had anything to offer her. He was only a former military officer, weak and wounded and now sidelined to life as a security guard with visible injuries to prove it.

Their eyes met, and her piercing blue gaze crashed like waves against his heart dredging up old memories. "You don't need me to tell you what happened." He shoved his hands in his pockets.

"Why not?"

Seth remembered her comment from earlier about the military. Now was the time to figure out what she knew about him. "Because you already know, don't you?"

Avery tried to act surprised, but she wasn't a good actress, and she clamped her lips.

"Am I supposed to know you from somewhere?" he asked. "Did you change your hair and add colored contacts or something when you went into witness protection?"

She shook her head. "No. We never met in person, but you knew someone very dear to me."

A tear slid down her cheek, but she quickly blinked, and the sorrow disappeared.

"Who is it?"

"Was." She stated the past tense matter-of-factly. "Logan Thompson."

The name hit his chest like a ton of bricks, and he found it hard to breathe. Logan's face filled his mind and tried to draw him back. Seth gasped for air and coughed.

Avery moved to his side in a moment and patted his back. "Are you okay?" she asked, her eyes wide.

"I'll be fine." He sat down on the yoga mat sprawled out on the floor and gave her a thumbs-up. "How did you know Logan?" The name sounded foreign on his tongue, unspoken for a long time.

She sat down across from him and waited a few seconds before answering. And he wasn't sure he wanted to know the answer.

"He was my brother."

Now it made sense. He recalled seeing pictures of Logan's sister alongside their parents in photos in his bunker. But they'd all been younger back then.

"He was in your platoon. Following commands given by your station." The words came out a whisper.

He tried to let her words roll off him, because she was hurting. Her brother had been killed. And although he blamed himself for those men's deaths, more to the story lay hidden behind the surface of what met the civilian eye. And Avery simply found someone to hold accountable for what had been taken from her.

"I'm so sorry." He couldn't bear to share more right now. "That mission lives engrained in my memory, and it cost me greatly. I lost a lot that day. And the reminders are constant."

This time, she stayed quiet. "I didn't know."

"There's a lot that people don't know about that time."

"I see."

He didn't like having this conversation. His legs itched with readiness to move on from the discussion. "So, your last name is actually Thompson?"

Avery nodded. "They let me keep my first name though. I'd already lost my brother. I didn't want to lose another piece of our identity that held us together."

The emotion in her tone was raw. She understood loss too. It proved a common denominator for many. Yet she'd run toward God and back to her family, and Seth had begun to question God and left most of his family. His brother was the only one who hadn't questioned him for what happened when he'd been discharged.

The alarm on his phone went off, and the vibration pulsed against his wrist.

"What's that for?" Avery asked.

"No one has contacted us, which means something could be wrong."

They both stood. Avery slipped back into her tan jacket.

"I'm coming with you," she said adamantly.

"I'd feel better if you stayed out of sight." He stood a little straighter. Now that she'd revealed her real identity and story, he wanted to ensure her safety even more. He owed that much to Logan. Take care of his little sister in his absence.

"And let you get hunted down only for them to come find me after they take you out? Not a chance."

Her statement cut like a scalpel to his wounds, affirming his deficits.

"Right. Two is better than one."

He opened the door and took the lead, not wanting to give anyone a chance to take her out without going through him first.

If something happened to Derek or Grant, Loki would have barked like earlier.

Unless… "Is this basement soundproof?"

"Not that I'm aware. Why?"

"All right, let's go. I don't like how long it's taking them."

They turned the corner to walk up the steps.

Glass shattered, and Avery screamed as her hand clamped down on Seth's forearm.

Pain ricocheted through his head as an explosion rocked the ground. He twisted and wrapped his arms around Avery's waist and dropped to the ground. Seth shut his eyes, and the images flooded his mind. Something wet oozed under his hand. Except he wasn't in Iraq and that sticky substance indicated Avery might be wounded.

SIX

Avery braced her hands along the steps so she wouldn't fall as she reoriented herself while the noise reverberated through the stairwell. The momentum of Seth's pull caused her to dig her fingers deeper into his skin, and something slimy covered her palm. Blood smeared along Seth's arm.

"You're hurt." Avery used the edge of her shirt to dab at the spots where he bled. She'd injured him. Avery pressed against the wound and averted her gaze, unable to watch his face cloud with disdain at what she'd done.

"I'll be fine." Seth hooked his thumb under her chin and lifted her face up. "It's a scratch. A paper cut, really. It'll heal quickly." He smiled. "Are you okay?"

"Mmm-hmm," she said.

The look of determination in his eyes sent waves of comfort down her spine. Seth pulled out his gun, keeping it low to the ground.

Where had the explosion come from? It sounded as if it had entered from the kitchen area, but she couldn't be certain.

Seth grabbed the doorknob.

"Wait." She touched his shoulder. Despite this man's connection to an unpleasant past, she didn't want him to get hurt. His eyes searched hers. Tears threatened to bubble to the surface, but now was not the time to give in to hysteria. "Please be careful. There's no knowing what's on the other side of that door."

"I know." His face turned solemn with the stark reality.

He moved his hand along the lower part of the door, touching different areas to make sure it wasn't hot. Then ever so slowly, he opened it.

Avery held her breath. And let out a cough as smoke and the smell of gasoline permeated the air. She pulled her shirt above her nose and tucked in her chin as they walked through the hallway.

"Over there!" she shouted, unsure if her voice was of any benefit to Seth. Flames licked at the floor of the dining room as heat emanated. "We've got to put it out."

Avery bolted for the kitchen before giving Seth a chance to say anything and grabbed the fire extinguisher from under the sink.

She raced back to the room and took note of

the shattered window. The outside air now fueled the flames as they climbed higher along the wall and carpet. Someone had thrown a makeshift bomb of sorts into her house. Her *safe house.* Anger bubbled inside her chest like the roar of the flames around her.

Avery pulled the pin on the extinguisher hard.

"We don't have time to tend to this," Seth said. "We need to get out and find the guys." He coughed. The smoke intensified and began to infiltrate the space.

"I have to at least try."

Seth's eyes narrowed. The only part of his face still visible with his makeshift mask. "Fine. You've got two minutes to get out." He tapped his watch. "I'm going to find Grant."

He made a beeline for the back door, going out to confront the person who wreaked havoc while she fought to contain the damage inside.

In a swift motion, she aimed at the base of the blaze and squeezed. Creamy foam spewed from the canister and coated the ground as it squelched the flames.

She raced back to the kitchen and filled a bucket with water, keeping her eyes fixed on the other room. Water soon overflowed onto her hands, and she grabbed the container.

The liquid splashed on the flames, and they began to sizzle out.

Her lungs heaved, and she let out another cough, unable to hold her shirt above her mouth and nose.

One more bucketful. She turned toward the kitchen, and a gunshot rang out.

Avery dropped the bucket, and it clamored to the ground. She moved to the back door and leaned against the frame listening. Her pulse thrummed in her ears, and she closed her eyes for a brief moment to calm her nerves. She needed something as a weapon.

The fire extinguisher would suffice. She clutched it once more, then slipped out the door and scanned the backyard. No activity presented itself, and Avery waited, deciding what to do.

She followed the edge of the landscape, with her back to the bushes as she approached the corner of the house. The large cylinder of metal stayed tucked to her side as she peered around the siding.

Male voices came from the front yard, but she couldn't make out who they belonged to. She took each step gingerly, as if her shoes would make noise on the soft grass, and rounded the corner.

Seth hovered over someone sprawled on the ground. Another person stood with a gun pointed at the ground, but Avery could only make out their back profile. The man slid the barrel back and turned the gun. Avery's breath caught in her throat as everything unfolded.

"Seth," Avery screamed.

Loki barked at her alert.

Both men turned their gaze, and Grant extracted the magazine from the weapon.

She dropped the extinguisher and jogged over to them.

"You're okay," she said with relief, and embraced Seth in a hug. He smelled of sweat and smoke, but he was breathing. Suddenly she realized what she was doing and took a step back and focused on rubbing Loki's forehead. "The gunshot went off, and I thought…" She peered up at them. "Where's Derek?" She hopped up and spun around but didn't see him anywhere in the yard.

A knowing look crossed Seth and Grant's faces.

"No." Her eyes widened, and she pressed her fingers to her mouth. "Where is he?" she cried.

"I'm sorry." Grant hung his head.

Seth's hand took hold of hers, but she jerked out of his grasp and walked away. There at the side of the porch lay Derek. Avery turned aside, unable to process that he was gone. Someone who'd fought for her safety.

She walked back over to the guys and remembered the other person in the grass who Seth towered over. "Is he. . .?"

"The one who hurled a Molotov cocktail into your house." Grant stepped forward.

Avery took one glance at the man and turned away. Blood seeped from his wound. The pale color of his skin was too gruesome for her to swallow.

"Do we need to call an ambulance?" she asked.

"Make that the coroner," Seth said, his lips pinched.

"What happened?"

"When we came out to investigate, no one was in the car. He was already scouting the area and must have snuck up on Derek. I didn't even hear the shot. When I found him, it was too late. That's when I noticed the guy. He had a lit bottle in his hand and chucked it through the window. I told him to put the weapon down, but when he aimed his gun, I had to pull the trigger." Grant rubbed his forehead.

Weariness invaded Avery as the adrenaline slowed, and she wanted to collapse on the couch with a hot cup of tea and curl up with a good book to discover all the events in her life were simply figments of an author's imagination for the characters.

Instead, the sun beat down on her face, the

harsh rays a reminder that real life played out in front of her as the attempts on her life continued to escalate.

She pinched the bridge of her nose. "I need to call the US Marshals. Let them know what happened."

Grant raised an eyebrow, but Seth didn't say a word.

"First, I'm going to need you to try to ID this man," Grant said.

"Right. I suppose I can do that." She pulled in a steadying breath.

Seth closed the gap between them and took his place at her side. Avery shifted to look at him, and he gave her a small nod, as if telling her she could do this.

The man stared up at her, his eyes haunting and cloudy. His features remained stoic, his jawline set. And his upper body was pure muscle. Although she'd never gotten a good look at her attacker's face, she suspected based on his strength that this was the same guy.

She concentrated on his face, willing a name to come to mind. Her eyes trailed down to the snake tattoo on his inner arm before her gaze moved to the chest wound. Her breath hitched. The world around her shifted on its axis.

Avery shuffled her feet and planted them firmly on the ground to keep from falling over.

She'd recognize that tattoo anywhere. Antonio kept his men hidden around every corner. Avery's fingers began to tingle, and her heart skipped a beat. She didn't want to remain a victim. The independent life she once lived continued to become a distant memory. She needed to regain composure, but the thought of living under marshal protection forever or, worse yet, being killed in the process prevented oxygen from entering her lungs.

The quest to silence her had just begun though. Because even if Seth managed to take out one guy, they'd send someone else to finish the job.

Avery looped a few strands of hair around her finger until it dug into her skin and cut off the blood flow. The reality of life's circumstances built until everything around her turned hazy and white dots flashed against the landscape.

Evil gained the upper hand, and Avery needed to find a way to turn the tide and soon.

Avery's frame crumpled, and Seth lunged forward to grab her arms as she melted into his embrace.

"Get her some water." Seth turned to Grant, who headed into the house.

Her skin emanated heat upon contact with his hand. Wisps of her hair cascaded around her shoulders and brushed against his skin. The featherlight touch tickled him. Even with sweat covering her brow and dirt specks dotting her skin, she looked innocent and breathtaking.

Avery's eyelids fluttered open, and this time, it was Seth's turn for everything around to fade away, as if they were the only two in the world.

"You know, you really need to stop making a habit of this," he whispered into her ear.

"Yeah, well, it's not every day someone tries to kill you."

He wanted to take her hand in his and tuck her under the fold of his arm. Instead, she slid onto the grass to create distance. His desire came like a bullet that barreled into a Kevlar vest and stunned him.

He needed to get his act together. This was Logan's sister. He was simply looking out for her, making sure she stayed safe. As a way to pay his friend back when he'd given the ultimate sacrifice.

He wouldn't permit feelings to invade. Because the moment they did, his guard would be down, and the cost of her life was too great to entertain even a blip in his resolve. He shuddered. No, he couldn't let himself get entangled in romance ever again. Not after a woman who claimed to love him had left him because he would never measure up to her picture-perfect standards.

"I don't even recognize the man." Avery broke the silence and tucked a piece of hair behind her ear.

"Hey, that's okay," Seth said. "Grant's the best in the field, he'll track down whoever it is."

"Did someone say my name?" Grant asked, walking over with three water bottles in his hand.

He tossed one to Seth and handed the other to Avery.

"Thanks," she said and took a few sips.

"I was just telling Avery here you're the best at solving John Doe identities."

"It's all part of a puzzle that has to be solved. I take it you didn't recognize the man?"

Avery frowned. "I wish, but no."

"Do you know what would have motivated this guy to attack?" Grant asked.

Seth opened his mouth, ready to ask a follow-up question about how they'd even been discovered, but the look on Avery's face silenced him.

He'd seen that expression before. One of utter terror. Knowing the outcome was grim.

She clearly didn't want to share information.

"If you'll excuse me for a moment, please." Avery stood up and walked to the far end of the driveway. She pulled out her phone but kept her back to them.

"You know something don't you?" Grant narrowed his focus on Seth.

"Bits and pieces."

"But you're not going to say anything, are you?" It had always been amusing how easily they'd been able to read each other's minds. They might not be twins, but the two had a special bond Seth was grateful for his whole life.

"It's not my place to say anything. As a cop, you should understand."

"I get it. But it's frustrating to know there are parts to the story that could help. Especially with two dead guys I have to explain to the PD." Grant raked his fingers through his hair, the ringlet curls bouncing around. "Do you even know what you've gotten yourself into?"

Seth steeled his gaze. "Yes. And I owe it to her."

"So, you already knew her?"

"Something like that."

Grant let out a sigh. "I'm only saying this because I'm your brother. You have nothing to prove. Whatever anyone says, you did the right thing. Just make sure you don't do something you'll regret."

Grant was right. But it was easier said than done, given the woman who stood in front of him. Avery moved her hand adamantly as she walked back and forth along the pavement.

His brother had supported him when he'd come back from Iraq, but what he didn't understand was that this time, he could amend for the mistakes he'd made. Actually show people his strength and capabilities.

Avery finished the call and walked back over, her steps punctuated and confident. She eyed Grant, who took pictures of the dead body, before returning her attention to Seth.

"Can we talk? Inside?" she asked.

He escorted her into the house and shut the door. The smell of burnt wood and fabric still strong in the air.

"Did you tell your brother anything?" Her eyes widened, and her chest rose and fell with each breath.

"Not yet. But he can help, Avery. He's one of the good guys, I promise."

"I know." The words escaped her lips with a sigh. "I just don't want anything leaked to the wrong people if too many others have intel on my situation."

"I hear you. The more people on guard and looking out for your safety, the better though. It'll make it harder for these men to get to you." Seth dropped his hands to his side. He didn't want to come across as too bossy or antagonistic.

"If my cover's blown, the marshals have one

option. Relocate me and intensify my security detail to where I can't go anywhere." Her words came out in a whimper.

If Seth wanted a chance to keep her safe, he needed to earn her trust. "I want to help so that doesn't happen. But I can't let you compromise on safety. It's one thing if Grant gives his expertise too. It's another if his life is in danger. I can't let him walk blindly into a dangerous situation," Seth added.

She chewed the bottom of her lip as she weighed his response. And if he were honest, the reaction was cute.

"Okay, deal." She extended her hand, and he shook it.

But Avery averted her gaze despite the quick exchange.

"We need to find a new place to stay."

"Wow, I'm flattered and all, but isn't that moving a little fast?" he said.

This time, Avery's face turned beet red, and she gasped. "That's not what I meant."

He let out a laugh. "I know. Just trying to lighten the mood."

She swatted at his arm. "Ha. Very funny. Since the safe house is compromised, the marshals are arranging for us to stay somewhere else." Avery wrung her hands. "They're also working on getting another handler since Derek…" She pulled in a breath.

"So, what's the plan?" he asked.

Avery's eyes glistened as a smile crossed her face.

"Do you recall the teacher's conference they're hosting on Monday for the week?"

"Yeah, but wasn't that switched to virtual because of the flooding at the retreat center?"

"It was. But I booked an Airbnb five miles from there and never canceled the reservation. I suggested it to the marshals, and they signed off for the interim."

"As long as the marshals gave you the green light," he said. No one would suspect them to still attend in person—or pretend to while they laid low.

"They're going to send another deputy out there to meet us. And Grant can keep an eye on things as well. The agency already confirmed that your background checks are fine."

Seth didn't have anything to hide, but the idea of someone looking into him sent a wave of nausea through his stomach. If he'd received the all-clear bill, maybe there hadn't been anything about his discharge.

"All right, then." Seth took a minute to fill Grant in on where they were headed. Once Seth was confident Grant had all the information he needed, he turned back to Avery. "Let's go."

"Thank you."

It was the first time she'd expressed her appreciation for his protection. Although he might need to clean his ears and have her repeat it. At least she acknowledged a need for someone to watch her back.

As they gathered their belongings, a nagging thought plagued his mind. They shouldn't have been discovered here. Which meant somehow, someone was keeping tabs on Avery, but he didn't know who the mole was or how they were doing it.

SEVEN

Trees blurred together as the car sped down the highway. One mile marker after another took Avery far away from the place she'd been told would keep her safe.

Avery leaned her head against the glass window. The AC blasted in Grant's car, and she tucked herself farther into the jacket she had on before sliding one of the vents closed. The silence of the car ride tempted her to drift into sleep. Good thing Seth insisted on driving.

Grant gave them his car in exchange for his motorcycle and promised to call with any updates he got on the dead guy.

In an Australian accent, the GPS told them to take the next exit in two miles.

"I forgot how far away this place is." Avery stifled a yawn.

"That's why we're stopping at a motel for the night."

"We are?" Avery shifted her head against the

window to get a better view of Seth. He had one hand on the steering wheel, the other resting comfortably on the center console.

"Figured it would give us both a much needed break. And make sure we aren't being followed."

"What?" Avery shot up straight and glanced at the mirror.

"Don't worry. Grant knows, and the marshals were informed of your location." He reached over to fold her hand in his. The gesture sent her stomach tumbling with butterflies, and her heart skipped a beat. She slid her hand out of his grasp. Those fingers caused too much damage and the early demise of her brother.

She didn't want to give any room for feelings. He was simply here, protecting her, out of duty to Logan. He said so himself. Thankfully, Seth hadn't displayed overbearing control like her independence threatened him. Yet past memories remained raw and refused to let her open her heart up to anyone else. One thing she learned too many times: waiting remained the key for time to show someone's true colors.

"I've been watching the cars. There's no tail. But I don't want to take any chances."

"Right." Avery eased back into her seat. "How would they find us though? How *did* they find me?" The question hung in the air as the weight of the havoc Antonio caused sucker punched her in the gut.

After they checked in to the motel and got their room keys, Avery opened the door, surprised at the spacious area. She set her duffel bag on the chair and surveyed the expanse of the room, which gave her time to stretch her legs.

"There should be another room on the other side of that door," Seth said, pointing behind her.

Avery tested the knob. Sure enough, the door opened and led into another space. The simple gesture warmed her inside, and she appreciated his concern for both of their integrity.

Her stomach growled. A reminder that she hadn't eaten anything substantial since early this morning.

Seth brushed past her and dropped his belongings off in the other room before coming back over and sitting down at the table in front of the TV.

"You want to order takeout?" Seth waved the handful of restaurant menus that had been on the table.

Call her selfish, but Avery didn't want to hide away in the room to eat. If she could have even a sliver of normalcy, she'd take it.

"You're certain we weren't followed here?"

"I'd say the chances are very slim."

"Good. Then to answer your question, no. Let's find a place to go eat." Avery's mouth watered. She wanted a juicy burger and sweet potato fries.

Seth scrunched his brows together.

She prepared to pull out the puppy dog eyes if he protested. Instead, he said, "All right."

They pulled into the parking lot of Glenn's Diner, the sign for the restaurant shone with neon yellow lights.

When they stepped inside, Seth let out a low whistle, and Avery chuckled. Everything was covered in yellow. The booths were yellow, the stools at the bar were yellow, even the servers sported yellow checkered aprons.

"They definitely have a favorite color," Avery said.

"That they do."

Once the hostess seated them and drink orders had been delivered, Avery stared out the window at the setting sun. Everything seemed peaceful, as if there wasn't a care in the world. People around them laughed and talked over their meals. What she wouldn't give to have that freedom again.

She supposed the old saying was true. You don't know what you have until it's gone. She sent up a silent prayer of thanks. Despite her current circumstances, she was alive. Although the fear crept into the crevices. Would she ever live a normal life again? Would she be able to come back and teach in the fall? Not being able to do what she loved sent a wave of emotion pummeling through her heart.

"What are you thinking about?" Seth stirred his straw in his glass of iced tea.

Avery shifted her focus to him. His brown eyes a chasm of never-ending depth. Like he stood ready to carry whatever burden she spoke out loud.

"Everyone else's life seems so normal from the outside."

"And you're worried it might not happen again for you?"

He read her thoughts so easily that it terrified her.

"What if I can't go back and teach because I'd put people's lives at risk?" She bit her lip to keep the tears at bay.

"A lot can happen in two months. And you've got a team of people helping you."

She nodded and took a sip of her Sprite. "You're right."

"Why did you become a teacher?" His question carried the weight of a thousand different answers, and she mulled over it, wondering how to keep it brief.

"I love helping people. Teaching them information and seeing their eyes light up when it clicks, and they finally understand it. It's such a satisfying feeling."

"There was someone who did that for you, wasn't there?"

He was doing it again, searching deep into the depth of her heart and somehow seeking to know more of what she cherished. He actually cared about her as a person, and Avery wanted to share it all with him.

"Yes." She smiled, remembering those long-ago days. "I always had trouble reading as a kid, but it wasn't until middle school when I finally got diagnosed with dyslexia. I hated sounding out words and reading sentences. It was always a puzzle that never quite fit together in my brain." She paused and took another sip of her drink. "But I had one teacher who never gave up on helping me and who reminded me I could master reading. With the right tools and mindset, it wasn't impossible."

"And you'll get through this too. You've got the grit." Seth smiled.

The waitress came over with their food. Two loaded burgers and a side of sweet potato fries for her and regular fries for Seth. She thanked the waitress, and as the woman left, Avery's eye caught the images scrolling across the TV at the bar in front of them. A video of a tow truck pull-

ing a car out of the Little Penn Creek played as
cops surrounded the area. Their blue and white
lights flashed across the water.

Avery grabbed a fry and shoved it in her
mouth. But the rich, sweet taste turned to chalk
as a picture of a black-haired woman popped up
on the screen. Although the volume remained
muted, her eyes scanned the subtitles and she
almost choked when the phrase "suspected to
be dead" scrolled across the bottom.

She grabbed the edge of the table and coughed.

"Everything okay?" Seth asked as he half
stood in the booth, ready to jump to her side.

With a wave of her hand and a nod, he sat
back down. A sip of her drink dislodged the
food, and she pulled in a breath.

"We need to go now." Her words came out
sharp.

"What's going on?" Seth furrowed his brow
as he scanned the restaurant for signs of something being off.

"I'll explain in a minute."

Seth flagged down the waitress for boxes for
their food, but Avery didn't want to wait around.
She needed air. The image of the woman engrained in her brain suffocated her.

Dead.

The one word screamed at her. Haunted her.

No, it couldn't be.

She hadn't talked to Chelsea in years. But her friend couldn't be dead. Avery risked her life to get Chelsea help. Encouraged her to leave her drug dealer boyfriend and live a better life when she'd gone with her to confront Dominic. Except everything changed the night of the murder.

Avery stood up and rushed past a couple being seated.

Seth called her name, but she bolted out the door, the night air rushing up to meet her face. The marshals pledged to safeguard people. So how did these men find Chelsea too? How had they gotten past the best protection detail in the country?

Seth grabbed the to-go bag from the waitress and mouthed a thank-you as he dashed out after Avery. He didn't want to leave her alone for a second, because anyone could stay hidden, ready to pounce at the right moment. Even though he was confident they hadn't been followed, he didn't want to take any chances.

Something clearly alarmed Avery about the news coverage. Her face had grown white as she'd stared at the screen, her eyes locked on the newscaster as if she'd been transported back to another time. A scenario he faced when a door slammed or fireworks exploded.

The overhead bell jangled as he made his

exit and scanned the parking lot. Up ahead, Avery jiggled the handle of the car as if she had enough force to open the locked door. In defeat, she turned around and braced her back against the metal before burying her face in her hands.

Seth paused to make sure nothing set off his sixth sense and took a moment to gather his resolve. Seth tapped his foot against the ground. He'd never been good at handling emotions, especially a woman's. After all, he hadn't had any sisters growing up.

Nothing he said or did would provide support right now. Not when her life had been unraveled and she'd been forced to run.

"It should be unlocked now," Seth said as he approached. She pushed away from the car and wiped a finger across her eyelids.

He took the opportunity to open the door for her.

"Thanks," she said and slid in.

Except for the hum of the engine, silence filled the ride back to the motel.

He escorted her into the adjoining rooms, and she plopped down on the sofa. She grabbed a pillow and hugged it tightly. Seth sat down next to her but waited for her to speak.

"They killed her." The words sliced through the silence, their finality honest and brutal.

"Who did?" he asked softly, knowing this situation impacted her greatly.

"Antonio and Dominic. And whoever else they have working for them."

"And who did they kill?" The words sounded harsh on his lips, but he couldn't think of a less direct way to ask what she'd already stated.

"Chelsea." Avery sucked in a breath. "That was her picture on the screen. Wherever the marshals took her, Antonio's men and her ex-boyfriend Dominic found her. And now they're doing everything they can to get to me."

He could sense the fear in her voice. The independent, self-sufficient woman he'd first met now sat with her shoulders curled inward; her gaze focused on the floor.

"Avery." He reached out and touched her forearm. "Look at me."

She reluctantly lifted her gaze to meet his.

"I'm not going to let that happen." Speaking the words out loud sent a rush of determination through his veins. He'd do whatever he could to make sure no one laid a hand on her. He hadn't been able to protect Logan, but he could make it right this time. "And you're a strong-willed woman, who fights and doesn't let fear win."

Avery sat back a little straighter. Her eyes glistened at his comment. He meant the words he'd spoken. Seth admired her sheer determination, and it attracted him. Needless to say, it could end up to his detriment. The moment she took to heart the truth of those words and recognized his shortcomings, she'd hightail it as far away from him as possible.

He went to stand up, but Avery rested her hand on his shoulder. "Thank you. I needed that reminder. We're not going to let them win."

"Now you're talking." He pushed himself off the couch. "We need to fill the marshals in on this new development."

"I know. I want to find out what happened. People don't just get killed under federal protection. There's something else going on." She propped her fingers under her chin.

"We should tell Grant too."

"Agreed. Although it's more digging and work he'll have to do."

"That's his job—to get to the bottom of it. Grant's got the manpower and access to resources."

"I want this nightmare to end." She flung her hand in the air. "I feel bad enlisting so much help."

"Given the circumstances, reinforcements aren't bad. Especially since I've got…" Seth didn't want to finish his sentence. Although she needed to understand a team remained the best option. Not him flying solo. He paced the length of the area between the door and kitchenette.

"And you what?" She steeled her voice, waiting for his response.

"I've got limitations." He dropped his hands to his side.

"Your limitations aren't a hindrance." The words rolled easily off her tongue like she didn't hold any of his mistakes against him.

Seth wanted those words to soothe his heart, but the reminders of his failures over the years added to his pessimism, and he couldn't help but hear an unspoken *yet*. They're not a hindrance *yet*.

"I appreciate that. But it's not fully accurate." The waterfall of words gushed forth, and he found himself reasoning with her as to why he wasn't the total package. "Growing up under the shadow of an older brother was hard. Grant excelled at everything—sports, academics—you name it. I could never measure up. He received all the praise, and I was always reprimanded for not doing enough. Not working out enough to make the soccer team, not spending enough time studying to get straight A's." He rubbed his jaw; the stubble scratched his fingers. "When I got discharged from the Army, my parents couldn't understand why I hadn't just found a job and become successful like Grant."

Avery stood up and closed the distance between them. "I can't even imagine. Although you're the one who stitched up my side and prevented a kidnapping. I'd say that's a pretty good track record."

"Did you just *thank me* for saving you?" He raised an eyebrow.

She let out a chuckle. "Let's just say I'm learning there may be more to you than meets the eye."

Before Seth could press her for more details on what she meant, a ping alerted him to a text, and he opened it. "Grant says he's getting the ID of the man at your house expedited. Since they found a phone on the dead guy, they're going to see if that turns up any leads."

"Tell him thanks. And ask him if he can find anything on a Chelsea Watkins."

"Are you sure?"

"Yes, I need to know more." She shivered and rubbed her hands up her arms. In a split second, her eyes widened, and she whipped her head around the space.

"Have you seen my jacket?"

"What jacket?"

"The one I've been wearing this whole time. The tan one."

Right. He recalled her having it on earlier, when they'd gotten to the restaurant.

"I think I left it at the diner," she said. "We need to go get it." Urgency laced her words, and she'd already grabbed her purse.

"Why don't we call the restaurant, first?" He searched for their number, called them, then waited until someone could confirm it was there. Sure enough, they'd set aside a tan bomber jacket.

As they drove, Avery's foot kept a steady tap against the floorboard. "Can you hurry up?"

"What's so special about the jacket?" Sometimes he didn't understand the value women placed on fashion. It was just a piece of clothing.

"It was Logan's."

Oh. That changed things. He pressed down a little harder on the gas.

Seth went to take the turn into the parking lot, and the sound of gunfire erupted around them.

"Get down." He barked the order, and Avery complied, crouching on the floor.

He whipped the car around and pulled into a secluded area tucked away from the lampposts. This vantage point allowed him to see the flash of light from the bullets as they connected with the glass windows.

Right where they'd been eating an hour ago.

EIGHT

"What's happening?" Avery's voice sounded foreign in her own ears, her nerves on edge. She propped her arms on the car seat in an attempt to peek out the window, but Seth's hand on her shoulder stopped her short.

"Don't move," he said in a firm tone.

Someone shot at the restaurant. The place they had been before. The knot in Avery's stomach told her it wasn't a coincidence. She closed her eyes and pulled in a breath to keep the nausea at bay.

"This is Seth Brown. We have an active shooter at Glenn's Diner."

Avery shimmied in the small space on the floor as Seth talked into his phone. He nodded then said, "Good. If they can make it two that would be even better."

Seth pocketed his phone, and her mind swirled with what to do. She balled her fingers. No way would she let these people take the one beloved thing she had left of her brother. She needed to get the jacket before it got torn to shreds by bullets. If it hadn't already.

Her hand shook as she braced it on the door handle.

Another pop sounded before deafening silence. She pinched her eyes shut. It taunted her. Beckoned her to see if it was truly safe. Her hand closed tighter on the cool metal of the handle.

They couldn't sit idle. "We need to do something, Seth. Make sure no one is hurt."

"I know." The features of his face softened. "But I don't want you to become collateral damage."

He had a point. But the urge to do something, anything, to help grew.

Please, God. Don't let anyone be hurt on my account.

From her angled view on the floor, clouds covered the sky, void of any light, except the street lamps several yards away. Hopefully the last patron had gone home, and only the restaurant staff took shelter inside. The fewer bystanders around, the better.

"I'm going in. I need to make sure everyone's okay and retrieve my jacket."

At the same time she went to open the door, the car's lock sounded.

"That's too risky. I can't let anything happen to you. No way, not on my watch." Seth shook his head.

"We're sitting ducks here!" Avery shrieked. This man infuriated her. He needed to get his act together and realize the strength he possessed.

"You can't go out there. The Marshals will have my head if something happens before they get here," Seth proclaimed.

"And let all trace of Logan disappear?" When this was all over, she needed to know the full story of what happened during Logan's deployment.

With the flick of her finger, Avery unlocked the door and stumbled out of the car, the muscles in her legs protesting in pain as she stood from the crouched position she'd been in.

Sirens sounded in the distance and slowed her racing heart. Avery fixed her gaze on the restaurant, the front entrance now a shattered array of glass.

Seth continued to persevere and stay by her side, despite her protests that she could handle herself. And he did it in a way she wasn't used to either. Not to smother her but rather support her. She tucked away the observation to process later, even as her heart told her it was a good thing.

"You can come with me." She turned to Seth who now stood next to her.

Avery stepped around all the parking lot lights and did her best to blend in with the shadows.

Seth covered her back until they moved against the side of the building. The brick wall stuck to her shirt.

The sound of a voice stilled her.

"I already said they're not here." The words came out baritone sounding and angry. "Yes, it said she should be here."

Avery's mind spun, and she pressed a hand to her side, the bandage bulky under her shirt. What clued them in to her whereabouts? In a careful movement, she gingerly pulled her burner phone out.

She tapped Seth's shoulder and pointed to the device with a raised eyebrow. Were they somehow tracking her on the phone, or had someone tipped them off?

"We need to get outta this place," someone else said.

The voice sounded familiar, and Avery wished she could see who spoke.

"Cops are showing up, and I'm not about to get caught."

"If we show up empty-handed, they won't be happy."

"Let's regroup, then we'll be back. Next time she won't know what hit her," the first guy said in his deep voice, the words dripping with venom.

Seth gripped Avery's hand and put a finger to his lips. *We need to go.*

They were so close to getting answers, but Seth was right.

They had no way to tell the direction the men faced or if their guns hovered at the ready. She couldn't risk making her presence known. These men meant business, and if she became collateral damage, everything ended. She wouldn't be able to testify, and justice wouldn't be served. She refused to let that happen.

Sirens sounded, and patrol cars skidded into the parking lot.

Hurry up! her brain screamed. These men didn't deserve to escape. The urge to see them handcuffed pulsed through her veins.

They needed to move though. If the officers saw them hiding in the shadows, they might think she and Seth were part of the attack. She held on to Seth's hand and inched back, each step slow. She used her other hand to slide along the brick building as a guide in the darkened space.

Something touched her heel and clanged on the pavement. She froze, each muscle taut. A quick glance behind her showed an empty soda can. Avery wanted to groan. If people would simply pick up their trash.

"What was that?" one of them said.

"Dude, we don't have time to investigate. We need to leave."

"Hang on."

Seth yanked her arm and began to run. The guy rounded the corner.

"Hey!" he yelled.

Avery sprinted forward but her ankle twisted on the uneven pavement, and her hand flew out of Seth's embrace.

The man grabbed hold of her arm. "Get up," he snapped. His grip dug into her skin. Avery rose slowly before she dropped down again. Her response took the attacker by surprise, and in a single motion, she swept her leg clockwise and knocked him off his feet before connecting her palm with his face as he fell back against the asphalt.

He let out a grunt but didn't move.

She brushed her hands together, satisfied with her back sweep kick.

She stood up and came face-to-face with a gun. Her heart pounded in her chest as the other man pointed the weapon toward her with one hand.

He wore sunglasses and a hat, which made it hard to make out his features, but his finger moved over the trigger.

She told herself to breathe. Neither the officers nor Seth would let her get hurt.

"Cops are all over this place. If you shoot, they'll have charges against you for first-degree murder." Seth's voice came from her right, but Avery didn't dare move to see where he stood.

"Come with me, and I won't have to kill you."

"And let you do it later? Not a chance," Avery spat.

"Police! Drop the weapon." Officers clamored behind her.

She stared at the man a few feet from her, not wanting any distractions to give this guy an even greater upper hand. The man squeezed the trigger, and Avery dropped to the floor as hot lead whizzed past her.

The shooter turned and fled even as return gunfire met Seth's ears from officers. People yelled commands, and soon police dispersed to different areas. Some went after the guy while others rounded to the front of the building.

Seth dropped to Avery's side, and he held his breath. These men attacked the moment they found out Avery hovered nearby. And he'd been helpless. So close to her side, yet still too far away.

He had to make sure she was okay. And she would be. There wasn't any other option.

He leaned forward and nearly smacked his head against hers as she sat up.

"Did you get him?"

Commotion riddled the parking lot, but Seth didn't see the shooter. "I don't know. He ran off after he fired. Are you hurt?" Seth asked, assessing her for any signs of blood.

She shook her head. "I wasn't hit."

Seth let out a sigh and extended his arm to help her up. "What happened?" He searched her eyes, grateful she was alive without any other injuries. But heat crept into the tips of his ears, and he clenched his jaw.

"There was a dip in the pavement and I tripped." She gave him a side-eye like it was an obvious explanation, and Seth couldn't help the laugh that escaped. The lightened mood a breath of fresh air.

"What's so funny?" A small smile formed on her lips.

"Your feistiness. When something stands in your way."

"Ah. Well, I won't let people walk all over me." Her face sobered.

"Exactly why you need to be careful. Things can be replaced, you can't." His voice rose a notch. He tried to push off his attraction to her with little success. It was hard to imagine life without her in it. Seth raked his fingers through his hair.

"But I almost…" Her words trailed off as she studied something behind him. "Hey!"

Seth whipped around.

Someone slid along the ground in the dark against the back of the building. When their eyes connected, the guy pushed himself up and ran.

"Don't let him get away. That's the other shooter!" Avery yelled.

Seth bolted after him, trying to close the space between them, but the guy sprinted harder. A fence stood ahead that separated the property from a service road. The moment he climbed that fence, he'd be gone.

Seth pumped his arms and legs to close the gap. A dog's bark sounded next to him, and Loki barreled past.

"Atta girl," he said. "Go get him."

The man reached the fence and put one foot on the metal and pushed off the ground with the other. Loki jumped at his left leg, and a scream curdled the air as the German shepherd dragged him down. He let out a few choice words as he kicked and writhed to free himself.

Seth grabbed the man's hands and twisted them behind his back. "Care to explain anything?" Seth asked.

"They'll come back. And next time, she'll leave in a body bag." The man's breath wreaked of tobacco, and he jerked, but Seth held tight.

"Loki, release."

Grant made his way toward them, gun drawn and pointed. Another officer followed, weapon at the ready.

Loki backed away from the man but didn't take his eyes off him, letting out a low snarl.

"We've got it from here, thanks." The officer pulled a pair of handcuffs and clipped them on the man before switching places with Seth.

Certain the police had the man detained, Seth made his way back to where Avery stood only to find the space void of anyone. He quickened his steps. The place swarmed with cops now. Someone must have noticed her disappear.

His shoulders relaxed when he got to the front entrance, and Avery stood there waving her hands in the air as she spoke with an officer who blocked her way into the establishment.

"I just need to get my jacket," she pleaded.

"Ma'am, this is an active crime scene. No one goes in."

Seth stepped up next to the two and placed his hand on the small of Avery's back. Her lip quivered.

"I know you have to follow protocol, but could you go in to retrieve it for her?" The officer's gaze shifted between them. "It's cool out tonight, and the jacket holds sentimental value." Seth hoped his words communicated sincerity.

"All right. But don't go anywhere. I need to take your statement."

"Of course." He nodded.

"Thank you," Avery said, and turned to him. The creases on her forehead faded, and she took a step closer to hug him. Seth relished the tenderness of her arms wrapped in his embrace.

However, deep in his heart, Seth could see it wasn't meant to be. The baggage he carried shifted to the forefront each time he searched her eyes. Those piercing blue depths, just like Logan's.

Seth scanned the surrounding area as they waited, staying vigilant for any shadows or movement that seemed off.

"I don't like knowing the one guy got away," Seth said.

"That makes two of us. Although maybe the other one will talk." Avery's eyes glistened with hope.

"I doubt it. If anything, they'll try to find a way to pick him off before he's given a chance."

"Oh, I didn't think of that."

"These guys work for a major drug lord, Avery. Those cartels don't mess around when one of their own get caught." Seth shifted his stance to favor his left leg. "I admire your strength—I really do. But we need to work as a team right now. I can't have you running off and getting mixed up in cross fire. No matter how important that jacket is to you."

She stood up straighter. He could see the rebuttal on her face.

"Or you could go with the marshals, and I step out of the picture," he said. He wanted to protect her, but if she held on to her stubbornness, it would be better to hand her over to the professionals so he wouldn't have to watch if she did get hurt.

She placed her hands on her hips. And just like that, she stood ready to discard him and move on with her life.

"Here you go." The officer returned with the jacket in hand, breaking up their heated discussion.

"Thank you." Avery tucked it under her arm.

"I need to take your statement now," the officer said.

They spent the next several minutes relaying what they'd witnessed after they pulled up to the diner.

"Is there anything else you can think of?"

"Actually, I do recall something. It seemed odd." Avery furrowed her brow. "The guy said *it* told them I was at the diner."

"Like a tracker?" Seth probed.

"Exactly."

"Can I see your jacket?" Seth asked.

He held it up to examine.

"There." The officer pointed to a black dot that sat under the armpit area. Completely out of view and unsuspecting.

"Now we have our answer." Seth pulled it off and held it.

"How did they put it there?" Avery asked, confused.

"The attempted kidnapping," Seth whispered. "They had you literally in the palm of their hand but weren't going to take any chances."

Avery gasped.

"This whole time, I've led them to my location. The house and…" She pulled in another ragged breath, and Seth worried she might hyperventilate.

"This is helpful information, miss. Now that we found the tracker, they won't be able to follow you," the officer said.

Seth dropped the bug on the ground before connecting his foot until it lay fragmented.

"Excuse me, I'm looking for Ms. Sanford." A man approached them in dress pants and a shirt.

Seth didn't recognize the gentleman and took a step toward Avery, just in case.

"You're speaking with her," Avery said.

"I'm Deputy Marcus Johnson." He displayed his gold-coated star badge. "I've been reassigned to your case." He extended his hand, and Avery reciprocated the pleasantry.

"Your cover has been significantly compromised, Ms. Sanford. We need to leave at once."

An unmarked sedan sat in front of them, and the deputy put his hand on Avery's back to usher her into the waiting vehicle.

"Wait." Seth took a step forward. Avery turned, her eyes wide.

"We don't need any more interference," Johnson snapped back.

The door opened, and Seth ran to the front of the car, his hands braced on the hood. He'd make them run over him before he gave up protecting her.

NINE

The pain in Avery's chest came like a weighted blanket suffocating her airway. She dug her heels into the ground, the effort met with resistance as Johnson tried to urge her forward into the car. This man might wear a gold-star badge, but she knew nothing about him. And it was growing harder to trust people.

"We need to talk," she said.

"Absolutely. But not here in the open," Johnson stated.

"I'm not leaving without him." Avery pointed at Seth. His stance in front of the vehicle told her he meant business.

And she liked it.

Maybe even liked him. A man willing to sacrifice for her. And he looked good while doing it, with those broad shoulders and sturdy hands ready to aid in defense.

Avery propped her hand on the door frame

and stood still, not giving Johnson the satisfaction of climbing inside.

Even with his admirable attributes, she could never fall for Seth. Not while they were still in danger. Especially not with their connection to Logan as a common denominator.

"You want to leave, you'll need to get through me first." Seth tilted his head.

"I'd like to talk here before going anywhere," Avery said.

The deputy moved his head side to side.

"Please, I just need a minute." Avery bit her lip. The stark reality that Derek Haynes, the deputy marshal assigned to her until after this trial, was gone for good hit her. The safe life she'd experienced for almost three years upheaved like a sudden gale of wind that blew through and tossed about anything in its wake. She pressed her fingers on the bridge of her nose to compose herself.

"All right. We stay here though, with a quick escape if necessary."

"Okay." Avery complied.

She wanted to warn Marcus about what he had walked into. But when he signed the contract to work in the US Marshals Service, the risks were communicated. She just prayed no one else got hurt at the expense of wicked men.

Avery couldn't tell if Marcus was older than

Derek or if the demands of the job had aged him with the gray specks peppered throughout his beard and a set of wrinkles etched into his face. His features reminded Avery of her dad. Another wave of sadness crashed over her. Despite the enjoyment of independence and not always getting along with her parents, she missed them. Especially the jokes her dad made on a whim.

"I know you've experienced a lot in the last few days. Although it will be helpful to run through all the details to put together the big picture."

"What do you need to know?" Avery asked.

"Who from the drug ring are you able to ID?" Marcus pulled out a notepad.

"Antonio Chavez and Dominic Trevino."

"Mr. Chavez is currently in custody, but Trevino is still at large. Do you know anyone else who would be doing their dirty work for them?"

"I don't know. I recognized the snake tattoo on the man who attacked my house. It's the mark of their ring. But I'm not sure who he was with. His name, I mean," Avery recalled.

"I see. Any idea on the potential kidnapper or men from tonight?"

Avery dropped her shoulders. "I wish I could give you more concrete answers, but I'm not sure. The one voice sounded familiar. Maybe it was the same person who tried to kidnap me or a different member."

"Well, we have one more in custody from tonight, and your attacker's body to ID. Something will come up." He smiled almost to make her feel better for her lack of knowledge.

"I hope sooner rather than later." Avery tucked herself into Logan's jacket. The temperature cooler now that the sun had made its descent. What had it been like for Logan in enemy territory? And would these people succeed in capturing her first before the trial? They'd somehow gotten to Chelsea. "Do you know how they located and killed Chelsea?" Curiosity took over despite Avery's uncertainty about discovering the answer.

"I'm not certain." He shook his head.

"If you can't share specifics, I understand," Avery followed up.

"She technically wasn't in our jurisdiction, so I'm not breeching any confidential information."

"What do you mean?"

"Unfortunately, she opted out of protective services." Marcus frowned.

Avery swallowed hard. She didn't expect to hear that news. Her former friend chose not to go into hiding? She'd been terrified of what Dominic might do to her. The risks involved were far too great, and she'd paid the price.

"I don't understand. Chelsea was petrified after what happened that night."

"I'm sure that would cause great trepidation for anyone," Marcus said. "But I've seen my fair share of individuals who don't want to change everything about their lives and pretend to be someone else. In a new place with a new job and name. It's a significant transition."

"I know," Avery whispered. "Are my parents still okay?" The lack of contact ate at her.

"We've never had anyone who followed marshals' guidelines ever get hurt." Marcus swiped his hand through the air in affirmation even as he avoided answering her question.

He must have taken note of her apprehension after the news of Chelsea.

"I hope so," she mumbled.

"There's another safe house set up we're going to take you to with heightened security."

Avery glanced over her shoulder at Seth. Relocating again reminded her of a nomad's life. Would they bring Seth too? He'd become a familiar face in a sea of changing tides. She wasn't sure she could handle being in confined quarters with him. Although it would be nice to have someone else to talk to and make the place less lonely.

"But there is one thing I need to ask first." Marcus's voice pulled her back to their conversation. His brow scrunched up.

"Of course. What is it?"

"Is there anyone who would possibly leak information on your whereabouts?"

The question left a bitter taste in her mouth. She hoped the answer was no. Her mind worked through the events of the last few days; each scene played like a reel as she tried to remember who she'd been around.

"Well, my school picture was leaked. However, I don't know if that was an error on an administrator's part or if it was intentional. It was taken down, right?" Her palms became sticky and clammy despite the cool night air.

"Yes. We received confirmation that it was removed and is now inaccessible."

"I think that's how they tracked me. Aside from the planted device so they could follow if they somehow failed to capture me. So, no, I don't believe there's anyone who would do such a thing."

"Not even him?" Marcus pointed at Seth.

Avery let out a gasp, appalled that he would accuse him of such a monstrous crime.

Seth glanced between them. "Excuse me?" he asked, without any hint of hostility in his tone.

"I was just asking Ms. Sanford here how she knows you and if you'd have any reason to share information about who she is with those who want her dead."

Seth's eyes went wide, and his cheeks turned pink under the street light.

"That's absurd," she interjected. Seth might play a role in her past, but she trusted him. He'd ensured her safety more than once, which counted for something.

"Then I want to know exactly how you know him and why he's tagged along, considering the several attempts on your life, Ms. Sanford." Marcus spoke firmly and crossed his arms.

Seth couldn't believe the accusations that dripped from the man's tongue. The deputy's gaze shot lethal darts. In a matter of seconds, Seth no longer stood in the parking lot of Glenn's Diner. Instead, he came face-to-face with his parents, who expressed their disapproval at his choices and failure to succeed in the military after his discharge.

He'd tried explaining his injuries and discharge were a matter of protocol—and an honorable one at that. It didn't matter; their expectations for him were destroyed.

Now this deputy wanted to interrogate him on false allegations. As much as he wanted to protest, raising his voice and getting defensive would only make him appear guilty.

"We work at the same school. I got her to safety when her car exploded," Seth stated.

"The last time I checked, saving someone's life was praised."

Marcus looked at Avery for confirmation.

"What he said is true. He intercepted the guy who tried kidnapping me. If he hadn't been there, who knows where I would be."

A shiver worked its way up Seth's spine as he considered what might have happened early that morning if he hadn't gone back to the wreck. "A background check was already done by the department and it came back with a clean record," Seth said.

With a wave of his hand, Marcus dismissed the information. "Yeah, we already covered our bases on that regard. I simply prefer speaking directly with people to hear the inflection in their voice. Decide if they're really telling the truth."

He really didn't like this man's disposition, acting like Seth was a menace. "I can assure you, sir, I want nothing but to secure Avery's safety."

"I'm sure you do. Ms. Sanford, do you have any comment to make?" The deputy directed the question at Avery but kept his focus on Seth.

She picked at a hangnail on her finger. "Well, I..." she stuttered. "His medical training came in handy multiple times. And he did destroy the bug these goons used to track us. So, I'd say he pans out just fine." By the end of her short speech, she spoke assertively, her feet planted on the ground.

Seth wanted to thank her but refrained.

"All right. That'll do." Marcus capped his pen and put his pad away. "You're a high-profile name right now, Ms. Sanford, and since you've been seen multiple times with her, you will come to the arranged safe house too."

Seth nodded, unsure what to say for fear of another explosive inquisition.

"We've got a decent travel time, so we need to get a move on." Marcus ushered them into the sedan.

Seth let Avery in first, then slid into the back seat. He made sure the middle seat remained open to give them both space.

Marcus climbed into the driver's side and checked the rearview mirrors before pulling out of the lot.

Avery leaned against the headrest and closed her eyes. A glance at Seth's watch told him neither of them would get rest anytime soon.

As they sped along the highway, Seth shifted his focus between Marcus and signs on the road to orient himself with the direction they traveled. His first impression of the deputy wasn't stellar, so it was going to take a while for this man to earn his trust.

Bright headlights shone as cars passed and weaved in and out of the lanes. Each one made him squint and taunted a headache on the horizon. It would be wise to follow Avery's lead and take a power nap. But brake lights lit up the area ahead where several cars stopped.

He'd never understand the amounts of traffic at all hours of the night. With a push of his arms, he shifted to sit up straighter in the seat, and his eye caught the high beams of a truck in the rearview. Except it wasn't about to stop. It barreled toward their car, the front lights encroaching upon them.

"Look out!" Seth shouted.

Seconds later a horn blared.

Avery jolted awake, and Marcus whipped the steering wheel to the right, but it was too late. Everything moved in slow motion as the truck rammed into their fender and pushed the car forward.

The vehicle went airborne. Avery let out a scream, but the squeal of tires drowned it out as they collided with something in front of them.

Seth's body jerked forward. The seat belt stopped the motion, and his head whipped back against the seat. He let out a hiss at the pain that tore through his neck.

Time ticked by. When nothing else happened, Seth unbuckled his seat belt then reached for

Avery's hand. It was hard to make out her features in the dark.

"What just happened?" she whimpered.

"I don't know, but we need to get out of here." He reached for her buckle and made sure it clicked. "Are you hurt?"

"I don't think so."

"Marcus, are you okay?"

Quietness mocked them in return.

"Marcus?" Avery leaned forward and tapped him on the shoulder. "Marcus, can you hear us?"

The deputy slumped over in the seat and his head drooped without any acknowledgment. Avery let out a cry at the response.

A sick feeling settled over Seth, but he didn't want it to be true.

"We need to go. Somehow, I don't think this was an accident." Seth almost choked on the words.

He tried the handle, but it wouldn't budge. He pushed harder and the door resisted. Seth refused to stay trapped in this car. Especially if a sniper lay nearby.

"Try the passenger door," Avery said.

He reached back and tugged Avery's arm as she maneuvered her way out.

Bystanders shouted and car horns blared. "Call 911!" someone exclaimed.

Once Avery got out, Seth jogged over to

the driver's side and yanked on the handle. It opened part way, enough for him to reach in to shake Marcus. The man's limbs flopped at the movement. His skin cool to the touch.

Seth stepped away and took in the scene. The truck that crashed into them lay disfigured a few feet away. There were too many people around with the potential to have ill intent.

"Someone just went around the back side of the truck," Avery said in a shaky voice.

"I don't like this." Seth guided Avery to the edge of the highway dotted with trees.

"What about Marcus?" Avery peered over her shoulder.

"It's too late. Medical personnel are already on the way and will take care of him." Seth quickened his pace away from the crowd, Avery's hand in tow. "We can't wait around to find out what will happen."

Avery flicked on her phone's flashlight, and the two took off into the overgrowth. They fumbled through brush and twigs, each step taking them farther from the scene. At least he'd paid attention while Marcus drove and had a general idea of the area. They needed to find a place to hide, but with two marshals dead, Seth wasn't sure who should be trusted or where to go.

TEN

Avery hugged the jacket to her chest and buried her nose into it, relishing the faint woodsy smell after a campfire. Despite all these years, it still smelled like Logan was sitting in the room with her. Except Logan was gone and she now hunkered down in a motel room trying to stay alive.

A tear escaped and slid down her cheek. She missed him. Their late-night chats, his laughter and the sparkle in his eye whenever a brilliant idea formed in his mind.

"Here you go." Seth handed her a disposable cup, steam rising from the slit in the lid.

"Thanks." She took a sip. The warm chamomile tea coated her throat and sent a cozy feeling coursing through her body. Although the drink wasn't the only factor that created a soothing effect. Seth continued to surprise her. What could it look like to be with a man like him? Someone who pursued her well and still let her be herself.

Avery cleared her throat.

Ambience or not, she didn't have time for fantasies right now.

Her muscles still ached from their trek through the wooded area. They'd doubled back to the restaurant to retrieve Seth's car before going back to the motel. It was a risk. Whoever hunted her might suspect she'd return. Although there hadn't been an ambush.

"You should get some sleep," Seth said and took a sip from his cup.

"And make you stay up all night?" Avery shook her head.

"That's why I've got the caffeine." He extended his drink in the air.

Avery wasn't tired yet. The events of the evening still haunted her mind. Including the voice of the one attacker. It pricked the edges of her memory, but she couldn't pin who. The lack of light and the way they'd concealed their faces hadn't offered any assistance in identifying them.

"We'll get an early start to the cabin in the morning. Make sure we don't have any more surprises along the way."

Avery let out a sigh. "I don't know how much more of this I can take." She rubbed her temples in hope of relieving the tension in her head.

Seth offered a grim smile but didn't say anything.

"I don't even know who to contact anymore." She groaned.

"This whole situation seems off. Like we're missing a significant piece of the puzzle." Seth propped his hands on his knees.

"You're right. Somehow, they've taken out two trained professionals." Avery choked on the words and blinked away tears.

"There's got to be someone on the inside feeding them information."

It had crossed her mind too. But how? And who? Could Marcus have been right about his distrust in Seth? He had been conveniently with her from the beginning.

His strong hands tenderly held the cup of coffee. The same hands that took care to stitch up her side. Certainly, he wouldn't be part of the plot to kill her. Seth had even surveyed every nook and cranny of the car to make sure there weren't any other hidden trackers before they'd made their way back to the motel. Which meant they should be safe.

As long as they arrived at the retreat center without any incidents, she would find a way to discreetly contact her parents and make sure they were okay. See if her dad had any insight on Antonio's cartel since he'd worked the case years before her eyewitness account. And find out if he had concerns about the marshals posted at their house.

"We need to keep our whereabouts on the down-low until we figure out who the mole is."

"Agreed," Seth said.

Avery studied him. His broad shoulders covered the space in front of the couch's armrest. The ceiling lights highlighted the scar on his face. His outer shell seemed tough, but she could see the brokenness on the inside.

"What happened with your convoy?" Avery rubbed the jacket between her fingers. "Did Logan tell you anything, before…" She couldn't finish the sentence, but the storm cloud that covered Seth's eyes conveyed his understanding of her unspoken words.

He hung his head and rubbed the nape of his neck before saying anything. "No one had an inkling of what would happen that day. You train for worst-case scenario, to always be on guard and vigilant. Yet there's something in your mind that says it could never happen to you."

Avery let out a short laugh, devoid of humor. She understood what he meant. From being a teacher and training to protect the students in an emergency with an intruder to now being on the run for her life. It became easier to block it out and imagine terrible things wouldn't come knocking on your front door.

"We were going into the village that day. Doing routine rounds to make our presence known. But it was also fun getting to engage with the towns-people. They were so friendly and kind. Especially the kids. Always ready to rope us into kicking a soccer ball around." As he spoke, Seth stared off into the distance, as if the memories were vivid once more.

"That afternoon, we headed back to our camp-site. Except we never made it." He paused. "One of the militant groups set up an ambush. There was debris in the road, and the first vehicle missed it, but the second didn't notice it in time and ran over it. The tires were flat pancakes, so everyone started loading what we needed into the other vehicles until shooting broke out."

She squeezed her eyes shut. The scene from the diner played on a loop in her mind.

"A mob of men rushed us from the hillside. I tried to radio the command center and cover my team's backs, but someone threw a grenade, and the area around me exploded." Seth got off the couch and just stood in the center of the room, his back to her.

Avery's heart broke at the sound of Seth's choked up voice. No, this man wouldn't try to kill her. Not with empathy like that.

A sudden urge to wrap him in an embrace invaded her emotions. Before she mustered the courage to go over to him, Seth continued, "I fell hard against the ground and couldn't make out any noises. Everything blurred. My side burned, and I could see the commotion, but I couldn't make out what was happening."

He'd been rendered helpless. His inadequacies laid bare in a moment when people needed him. The painful reality tugged at her heart, but she needed to know the answer to another pressing matter. For peace of mind.

"What about Logan?" Avery asked, her mouth dry.

Seth turned around and faced her.

"He rushed to my side and dragged me behind one of the convoys to keep us from getting hit."

"Was he injured?" Her hands cramped from squeezing the jacket. She could tell Seth debated how much to say by his pinched lips.

"I can handle the truth," she said.

"His leg wasn't in great condition as he army-crawled."

Avery took a sip of her tea, the calming effect no longer worked. "What happened then?"

Seth drew in a long breath. "One of the militants came up behind Logan. I saw the guy and tried to warn him, but another explosion rocked the air and drowned out the words. They dragged him away, and we couldn't locate him. I was responsible for his safety. Now he's another name on the MIA list, presumed dead." Silent tears cascaded in a steady stream down his face, and Avery wrapped her arms around him.

"I'm so sorry," he said into her shoulder.

Although she wanted to be angry with him and solidify her point that he'd been the cause of her brother's death, she couldn't. All those years, she needed someone to blame. But it wasn't Seth. His team trusted him as commander, and he'd done what he could in the situation. Because the reality of the matter was that Seth hadn't been in control. Evil men took advantage of an opportunity to execute the evil desires in their heart. Like those who hunted her now.

"I forgive you." The spoken words formed a balm over her heart and took away the resentment and bitterness she'd held on to for seven years over the unknowns of Logan's death. The truth of what happened and the torture he'd endured took a knife to her heart. But at least it provided the closure she longed for. Logan's body had never been recovered, and their chance to have a proper funeral had been stolen. Something her parents still grieved over.

Avery took a step back, her hands still on his arms. "It wasn't your fault." He needed to hear those words as much as she needed to say them.

He took her hand in his and placed a soft kiss to the outside. His gentle touch confirmation that her words soothed the rough edges of his heart. "Thank you."

She nodded, unable to say any more.

"You should know he loved you. He talked about you often. His face beaming with pride for his sister."

As Avery climbed into bed an hour later, she let Seth's words wash over her. Her brother had loved her, but hearing it confirmed brought comfort. It bolstered her strength for whatever lay ahead. Because he had been a fighter, just like her. And maybe, just maybe, having Seth on her team was a good thing.

The sound of clanging glass met his ears, and Seth shot up from his position on the couch, his hand instinctively hovering over his weapon holster. He turned toward the noise. Avery sat at the table, a bowl in her hand.

"Sorry," she said, a sheepish grin on her face.

Relief flooded him to know an intruder hadn't weaseled his way inside.

"How long was I out?" Seth stood up and stretched. A yawn escaped his lips.

"I've been up for an hour. Don't feel bad. You needed the rest too," she affirmed.

"I know. But that means anyone could have approached the room, and I wouldn't have known."

"Considering how quickly you jolted awake, I doubt it," she said, an attempt to console him.

He appreciated the gesture, but it didn't make him feel any better. "We should really get on the road. I don't like the idea of us staying here any longer." His face sobered.

Avery walked back into her room and reappeared a minute later with her duffel bag. "I'm all ready to go," she said.

He gave her a raised eyebrow as he picked up his own belongings.

"It's not like I had a need to unpack anything." She shrugged her shoulders.

Back on the road, silence filled the car. He kept an eye on the rearview mirror to make sure no one attempted to tail them.

So far, no cars hovered nearby.

The words Avery spoke last night still swirled through his mind. *I forgive you.* It rolled off her tongue so easily, and he almost didn't believe the authenticity of it. Would he ever be able to forgive himself for what happened? Let alone the Lord? Ever since the failed mission, he'd seen himself as frail. Incompetent. Every time he saw himself in the mirror, it taunted him.

God doesn't expect you to come equipped to the battle. Your insufficiencies let His glory shine through. The pastor's words from church last week echoed in his mind.

Avery extended him grace when she could have held a grudge against him. The one person who should have prevented her brother's disappearance and presumed death.

Yet, when he shared the full story, she did the complete opposite of what he anticipated.

He snuck a glance at her. She'd cinched her strawberry blond hair into a bun and rested her head against the window.

"How did you do it so easily?" He voiced the question that burned in his mind.

"Do what?" she asked, turning her head to look at him.

"Forgive me."

Avery let out a sigh. "I wanted someone to blame for losing Logan. But it wasn't your fault. It was the choice of sinful people carrying out their fleshly desires. And pointing fingers can't change the outcome."

"Despite my clear failure to find the strength to fight back?" If he'd just been able to get his body to cooperate. If he hadn't been so incompetent, things could have ended differently.

"You were injured, Seth. We all have moments of weakness."

And that's exactly what scared him. That in his moments of weakness, he'd fail to help anyone. Including the woman sitting mere inches from him. Someone whose company he'd begun to enjoy. But sooner or later, he'd mess up and she'd get hurt.

Before he had a chance to respond, his phone rang.

With a couple clicks, he accepted the call and connected it to the car's Bluetooth.

"Grant, what's up?"

Avery shifted in her seat and leaned closer to the dashboard.

"An ID came back on the guy up at Avery's house."

"You're on speaker, Grant." Seth nodded at Avery in a gesture to let her do the talking.

"What was his name?" she asked.

"Victor Tuliz. Does that name ring any bells?"

"Not that I can recall."

Seth shifted into the passing lane and sped in front of a tractor trailer that inched at a snail's pace up the hill.

"Okay," his brother said. "There were also some interesting messages on Victor's phone. I'll send you the full screenshots in a minute, but he frequently used the name Thunder Cloud. Do you know what that might mean?"

Avery sucked in a breath. "Thunder Cloud is the nickname Antonio goes by. I'm certain Victor worked for him."

"Who's Antonio?" Grant asked.

In his peripheral, Avery bit her lip. If they were

going to catch this guy, Grant would prove helpful. Except Avery didn't know his brother like he did. He trusted Grant, but with someone leaking information, he understood her skepticism.

She let out a sigh before saying, "The man who's after me."

"How do you know?" Grant's perplexed tone came through.

"Because he's the one I witnessed murder a woman."

A few raindrops splattered onto the windshield, the dark clouds overhead an indication of a dreary day.

"Which is why you're in WITSEC?" Grant asked.

"Yes," Avery confirmed. "He's in custody, but the rest of his gang is still at large, including Chelsea's ex-boyfriend, Dominic."

Seth turned up the volume a few notches to make sure he could hear Grant's voice.

"I see." Static crackled on the other end. "So you're confident that Antonio is Thunder Cloud?"

"Absolutely," Avery said. "I remember Chelsea mentioned it a few times. She was mixed up in drugs, and her boyfriend, Dominic, was supplied by Thunder Cloud."

"Thunder Cloud could be a code name for someone higher up on the totem pole," Seth said, thinking out loud.

"I doubt it." Avery shook her head.

"Did Antonio ever introduce himself by the name?" Grant asked, voicing Seth's concern. He didn't want to discount Avery's claims, but it was better to play devil's advocate to think through every possible avenue.

"No, but each member in the drug cartel has a tattoo. They all had some form of a snake on their bicep, except for Antonio. His is a lightning bolt coming out of a cloud that looks like it's striking a snake."

A sign of authority and allegiance. These cartels played no games. And somehow the woman who sat next to him had been in the wrong place at the wrong time. The horror of what she'd witnessed something he knew all too well.

"Okay. I'll keep digging on my end and see what else I can find. They can only get away with this for so long before they slip up somewhere," Grant said.

Seth could only hope it was true.

"One more thing," Avery said. "Have you found anything on Chelsea?"

"Nothing different than what the police report states about her death, but I'll keep looking."

The call disconnected, and Seth turned on the windshield wipers as the rain came down harder.

"I want to know how Antonio is communicating information from his prison cell." Avery scrunched up her forehead.

"You and me both. Although they have their ways."

They drove in silence for some time. Dark clouds loomed on the horizon, which hid the sun and made it a less than ideal summer day.

Avery stared out the window as they traveled down the road.

"How have you coped with all this? When you couldn't talk with friends?" At least he'd had Grant when he came home. They both had endured the struggle of starting a new life and what it meant to pick up the scraps and forge a different path.

Seth couldn't believe that a few days ago, he had no plans for his time off other than to relax and catch up on some projects around his house. Now he was on the run with this woman who he hadn't even spoken to until the other day. All because she'd left her lunch in the classroom.

And now his heart sat on a platter, ready to be served, should she accept. She'd forgiven him for the mistakes he'd made with Logan, and he wanted to take care of her. But the cost seemed far too great if he busted the mission. Could he be the man she needed without putting her life in jeopardy anymore?

ELEVEN

When Avery uprooted her life, all her friends disappeared. The community around her gone in the blink of an eye. She had no one to lean on. "It wasn't easy." She shifted to see Seth better in the car. His eyes held storm clouds like the ones outside and she wanted to erase and replace them with sunny days. "Sometimes I still don't think I cope well."

"Ebbs and flows?"

"Absolutely."

"I tried to keep life as normal as possible." She laughed. "I still had a job. Got involved in another church, kept up with karate." She remembered those first days of transition. Her own period of grief as everyone else's lives went on as usual, while she was thrust into a new environment.

"How did you get into karate?" He raised an eyebrow.

"It was a way to bond with my dad. My relationship with my parents wasn't the best growing up, but we shared that interest. He'd go to the gun range after work, and the karate studio was a block away. So afterward I'd show him all the moves I learned." She shrugged her shoulders.

"I'm sure he was thrilled to see what you learned."

"I think the real reason was it kept the boys away."

Seth let out a laugh. "That'll do it. Well, you certainly have the skills to fend for yourself."

A pop sounded, and Avery jumped. "What was that?" Her hand flew across the seat and gripped Seth's. His Adam's apple bobbed as he swallowed. His gaze trailed to her fingers wrapped around his before he turned his shoulder to look in his blind spot. "A car backfired."

"Sorry." Avery pulled her hand away and let out a sigh. "Everything makes me jump now."

"You and me both," Seth said.

The warmth of their brief touch hovered over her skin and sent her heart racing. The rain dripped down the window as the windshield wipers moved in a repetitive motion. "Could we stop at the gas station?" A sign up ahead indicated a stop for gas and restaurants at the next exit.

Seth's brow furrowed as he debated her request.

"I need to use the restroom." She rubbed her eyes as weariness invaded, which had nothing to do with lack of sleep. What she really wanted was to hear her parents' voices. Make sure they were okay. But that would prove a foolish decision, and neither Seth nor the marshals would approve.

"Can you wait until we get to the cabin at the conference center? We're not that far away."

Avery wrinkled her nose. "I'd rather not try that. And this way we can truly make sure no one's followed us or knows our whereabouts."

"Why's that?" he asked.

"Because they'd try something when a window of opportunity presents itself. Like being in the store unaware."

"I don't like the way that setup sounds, but you have a point." Seth flicked on his turn signal and took the exit before pulling into the gas station.

He maneuvered the car around the side of the building and parked by the dumpster.

"Really, the trash?" She wrinkled her nose.

"I'm looking out for your safety. Less conspicuous is better right now." His face shouted stoicism, and she could see how he'd once made a good commander. "Let's make this quick."

"Aye, aye, Captain." She saluted him.

"Are you mocking me?" He raised an eyebrow as they stepped out of the car.

"I would never," she said, even as her lips cracked a smidge. The banter smoothed the rough edges, like friends hanging out and enjoying the day. Not frantically watching their backs.

Friends.

She savored his company. But the reality was that after he finished his duty, he'd go back to living his life and she to hers. Especially once they hired a permanent security guard at school. This bond had been forged from protection and fighting for safety and nothing more. At least that's what she told herself. There was no way he'd actually want to be around her. Not when he probably pictured Logan in his mind every time he looked at her.

Wariness surfaced in his voice too. Her independence and ability to defend herself scared him. He wouldn't want someone who could hold their own. And it would end if he tried to box her in.

A display of greeting cards beckoned to her as Avery made her way through the aisle. "Give me one second." She held up a finger to Seth.

She picked up a card with a boat tied to the dock while hues of orange and pink reflected off the water. The picture took her back to sunny days with the family. She could write to her parents and let the marshals deliver it. Avery picked up the envelope with the card then made a beeline for the restroom.

Seth took his stance outside the door like a trained bodyguard.

She longed to know how her parents were doing. To look in their face and know they were okay. The pen hovered over the blank paper, taunting her.

This ordeal has put a strain on your father. An interference really. Her mom's words from one of their last conversations echoed.

Avery rubbed her temple. She never wanted to bring more heartache to her parents. Not after Logan's tragedy.

Every time you think you know what's best, it backfires and wreaks havoc. Avery could still envision her mom's frown and crossed arms.

A knock sounded on the door.

"Avery?" Seth called.

"One minute," she said.

She wished their words would roll right off her shoulder. In reality, they stung and prodded at the places where she didn't meet others' expectations. She didn't want to interfere. All she hoped for was to make an impact in peoples' lives. And somehow that caused more problems than solutions.

With a dab of toilet paper, she cleaned herself up, hoping the red streaks wouldn't be noticeable to Seth.

She closed the blank card and let it dangle from her hand. Avery opened the door and almost ran into Seth's back as his body blocked the doorway from anyone else entering.

"Whoa." She pulled up a step short. "I'm ready whenever you are."

He turned around and assessed her. His gaze trailed and stopped at her face. "What's wrong?" His hand extended toward her cheek, and no reflexive self-defense moves had the power to push aside this man's intuitive gesture.

And there in the middle of a no-town gas mart, the floodgates rushed open.

He'd seen the redness in her eyes when she'd walked out of the bathroom. Something wasn't right. Except now, a few customers walked by to grab drinks from the refrigerated section and gave them a look.

Unsure how to comfort her, he stood there for a moment as his hand hovered in midair. He half expected her to swat at his arm, like someone getting rid of a pesky fly. What could have happened in the matter of minutes she'd been out of his sight?

"Did something happen?" Fear gnawed at

him. What if these men changed trajectory and targeted someone close to her?

A hiccup escaped as she shook her head. She pulled in a steadying breath.

Seth took the pad of his thumb and wiped a tear that rolled down her cheek. He would give anything to carry her burdens for her. His heart ached with the desire to take away this pain and make her forget everything that was happening. Except he couldn't do that.

Not now, not ever.

He'd always be a walking reminder of what she lost.

Seth took a step back and laced his hands behind his neck. Now was not the time to add more emotion to an already intense moment.

"Sorry. I don't know what overtook me." She blinked several times.

"No need to apologize. You have a lot going on, and it's okay not to have it together all the time."

"I suppose so."

Her eyes scanned the store. This woman stayed in defense mode constantly. Prepared to take whatever came her way. But that pressure had to be a weight on her shoulders.

"What's the card for?" He pointed to the piece of paper she held in a white-knuckled grip.

"I wanted to write to my parents. But it was

a silly notion." Avery set the card on top of the candy rack.

Considering the number of tears and the distressed look on her face, he begged to differ.

"That's not silly. It shows you care," Seth said, then took in his surroundings. He would not be caught off guard again if someone attempted an attack.

"They don't want to hear from me anyways," she scoffed.

"Why do you say that?"

"My interference with Chelsea got us in this mess and destroyed my parents' lives a second time," Avery said as her shoulders drooped.

"Hey." Seth turned back to focus on her. "I wouldn't call it interference. You were helping a friend. There was no way you would have known what was going to happen that night."

"I just want to make them proud," she whispered. A sheen of moisture filled her eyes again. "To show them I am capable of accomplishing things. Doing tasks with grit, just like Logan. They were always so happy with him."

"Sometimes those closest to us don't express how proud they are in the best way. But I know they see how amazing their daughter is."

"They could do a better job of showing it." She let out a laugh.

The bell overhead rang and alerted them to a

new customer. Seth stepped off to Avery's side and pulled a bottle of water from the refrigerated case then grabbed a pack of gum from the display.

"Seth." Avery's voice near his ear sent a shiver down his spine. Her expression changed and a dark cloud covered her eyes. "Do you see the man over in aisle three?" The words were barely audible, and he focused on reading her lips to make out what she said.

She tilted her head to the left.

Seth studied the mirror mounted on the wall in the corner, which gave a perfect view of several aisles. How many attempted shoplifters had come through those doors before the extra measure of security had been installed?

It worked in their favor though, because sure enough, a man with a ball cap stared at something on the shelf with his head bent low.

"I see him." Seth confirmed but didn't know why it set off her alarm bells. "Did you notice anything?"

"His arm."

Her words continued to come out in a strained whisper, and he shifted his attention from the mirror to her and back.

The man wore a muscle shirt, his arms toned. Clearly, he either worked out frequently or took something to manufacture those muscles. Aside from being a gym buff, Seth wasn't sure what had Avery so concerned. Nevertheless, he shifted his stance to block Avery and continued to study the mirror.

The guy reached out to pull something off the shelf, and his inner bicep flashed for a moment. With a snake tattoo inscribed in colored ink.

Two more men approached the guy, and Seth let out a low grunt.

The guy in the ball cap pulled out cash from his pocket before handing it to them.

Snake. Seth mouthed the words, which certainly took on more than one meaning. Avery nodded in response. He grabbed her hand, and they walked down the farthest aisle away from the men. Their operation had eyes all over the place. It made him want to puke.

Something clattered behind them, and a guy shouted a few choice words, but Seth continued moving. Not taking the chance to turn around.

He remembered seeing a door at the side of the building when he'd parked by the dumpsters. The last thing he wanted to do was fend off three guys while defending Avery. Although her firm grip in his hand and the quick strides she made next to him indicated she could hold her own.

"I think there's a door back this way." He

dropped the water and gum on a rack. No time to make a purchase.

"Over there." Avery pointed to where the Employees Only sign hung.

He pushed opened the swinging door.

"Hey! You can't go back there," a woman exclaimed.

Seth ignored the comment and plowed forward. Sure enough, there was a door on their right with a big neon Exit sign displayed above it.

Heavy footsteps sounded behind them, and he spared a second to look back in time to see the man in the ball cap walk through the swinging door.

"Run," Seth said as he pulled Avery's arm.

They raced out the door and were greeted with a deluge of rain. He kept his head down as they bolted for the car.

Releasing Avery's hand, Seth ran to the driver's side. The lack of her touch left an empty void. But that would be nothing compared to the horror he'd feel if these men snatched her.

With a turn of the key, the engine roared to life, and Avery closed the passenger door as he peeled out of the parking spot.

A gunshot went off, and Seth swerved, zipping past the guy in the ball cap, who now ran to another car.

He pulled onto the road, and to his horror, the dashboard lit up with the low tire pressure symbol. They'd hit the tire. But there was no way to stop now, or he and Avery would be toast.

His hands stayed taut on the steering wheel. "Keep an eye on the back, please." He turned to Avery. "It's hard enough seeing what's in front of me with this storm."

"I haven't taken my gaze off it," she said.

"Good. I'd expect nothing less."

"Thanks." She smiled.

He turned the wipers on full blast. Now would be a good time to pray. Considering all the odds were stacked against them. But prayers didn't come easily to Seth these days. Especially when God answered in ways he didn't like.

"They're behind us now," Avery said.

All right. Now was the time to say something to God. Even if Seth was rusty and couldn't predict the outcome.

Lord, please help us. I can't do this on my own. I don't understand why You didn't save Logan and all those men that day in Iraq, but I could really use Your guidance now. For Avery's sake. Please don't let evil triumph again.

For the first time in a while, a weight lifted off his shoulders, as if admitting his shortcomings and relying on someone else's strength was okay.

When I am weak, then I am strong.

The words of the verse echoed in his heart in this moment of desperation, because he couldn't do it on his own.

A glance at the dashboard showed the tire pressure had gone down another five PSI.

He hoped they would make it out alive.

TWELVE

Nausea rolled around in Avery's stomach.

"I don't like how car chases are becoming a normal occurrence," she said and braced herself against the seat, the rockiness of the drive making her car sick.

"As long as we make it out alive, I'll take it," Seth said. He leaned forward toward the steering wheel, eyes intent on what lay in front of him. Without the headlights on, Avery didn't know how he could see much of anything.

Lightning lit up the area around them, giving them a short window of visibility, and thunder cracked the sky a second later. Storms always reminded her of God's power. He never abandoned her, but it didn't change the terrifying reality of the circumstances.

Her mind recalled the familiar verse from Psalm 23, and she spoke it over and over to herself as the cars followed behind them.

Though I walk through the valley of the

shadow of death, I will fear no evil: for thou art with me; thy rod and thy staff they comfort me. Thou preparest a table before me in the presence of mine enemies.

Yes, even in the midst of death knocking at the door, and enemies in hot pursuit, God was here. Was this how David felt when he'd run from Saul, who had made it his mission to kill David? The fear and angst. Knowing he needed to trust God, regardless of the outcome.

Trust.

The word slammed around her heart. That meant she'd have to surrender control and not rely on her own strength. To trust the Lord to shepherd and guide her.

Avery pushed the internal dialogue to the recesses of her mind to think about later. Right now, her body screamed at her to focus on survival.

"How long do you think we can make it on the tire?" she asked, almost too afraid to know the answer.

"As long as it takes to get away from these men." Seth gritted his teeth.

They were on their own right now. No marshals. No other protection detail. Had Chelsea experienced this same desperation when Antonio's goons found her and the chance of escape narrowed?

Avery focused on the rear and bit her lip.

"He's four cars behind us right now," Avery relayed. Maybe the rain would work in their favor, as traffic behind them moved at a snail's pace.

"The GPS shows a turnoff up ahead. Looks like a back road that runs parallel to the highway. Hopefully we can lose them that way."

"There's about to be an opening behind you. Get ready to gun it," Avery said, her body twisted in the seat to get a better view. "Go!"

Seth hit the gas and steered into the other lane before taking the off-ramp. The car bounced while zipping down the road. Would they survive an escape if they lost the tire or started hydroplaning?

Seconds that seemed like hours ticked by as she waited for the other car to emerge.

"Any sign of them?"

"Not yet." Avery let out a breath she didn't realize she'd been holding.

After a couple more turns down windy roads and no sign of being followed, Seth said, "I think we're in the clear. For now."

She lifted her eyes to the cloudy gray horizon and offered a prayer of praise, knowing things could have ended much differently.

Avery turned back in her seat, and the motion tugged at her side and sent pain through her abdomen. She winced.

"Your injury still bothering you?" Seth asked.

"Yeah. This posture isn't great for my side." She leaned back and pressed her hand to her wound.

Both of them stayed vigilant. Their attention shifted from the front to the rear.

Fifteen minutes later, Avery was grateful to see the cabin as they pulled onto the gravel road.

"Thank you, Jesus." Seth leaned back in his seat.

"I second that."

"Why don't you get settled inside, and I'm going to change the tire."

"In this weather?" Avery raised an eyebrow.

"There's a covering over there I can use." He pointed to a patch of tall trees that lined the front yard.

"Okay." Avery pulled up the keyless entry information on her phone and carried their bags inside.

A fraction of natural light worked its way through the windows in the entryway, and she used her elbow to flick on the hallway light. But nothing happened. Everything remained shrouded in darkness.

An uneasy feeling settled over her.

I will fear no evil: for thou art with me.

She repeated the words as she worked her way along the wall, looking for another light switch.

She glided her hand along the wall by the kitchen, until it connected with another switch. But nothing happened when she flipped it up and down. Avery turned on the flashlight on her phone and studied the area.

Nothing appeared out of place. The colors of the sofa and walls made the space warm and inviting. So, why wasn't anything working? She walked around the rest of the house, checking the two rooms and bathroom.

Another boom of thunder rattled the house. Then it occurred to her what might be the problem.

She dug around her bag until she pulled out the charging cord and plugged it into an outlet. When the phone didn't connect, it confirmed her suspicion. The electricity had gone out.

Once she donned her rain jacket, Avery stepped back out into the rain and made her way over to Seth.

He lowered the jack, and Avery stood a few feet away in his direct line of sight so she wouldn't startle him.

When he finished, Seth smiled up at her.

"Got the tire changed already?"

"It wasn't that hard," he said and threw the tools and old tire into the trunk.

"Well, I hate to break it to you, but there's something else that needs to be fixed."

"What's that?"

"The electricity's out."

"Of course it is," he said, grimacing.

"You think there's a generator somewhere?"

"Being out here in the woods? I'd say the likelihood is good."

They headed back inside, and Seth located the breaker box. "I'm going to check if they have a generator set up out back."

"Do you want help?" she asked.

"No. Stay where it's warm and dry, and if I need assistance, I'll holler."

Seth headed out the front door, and Avery paced the length of the living room, running through the list of information about the trial, Antonio, and Chelsea. Except it didn't feel like much.

Ten minutes passed, and the lights still hadn't come on, so maybe Seth had been unsuccessful. A shadow moved beyond the side window. Another minute ticked by and Seth didn't come back inside.

An uneasy feeling began to form. What if that hadn't been Seth by the window? It seemed he'd been gone an awfully long time. She'd rather see if he needed help than stand in here twiddling her thumbs. Avery zipped up her rain jacket and opened the front door.

The rain had turned to a light drizzle as she made her way through the mushy grass. Someone walked across the backyard by the tree line. But who?

Seth was hunched over a box next to the patio. She needed to alert him. If she whispered his name, he wouldn't hear. And if she walked over to him, whoever was by the trees would see her.

Avery reached for her phone but came up empty. Of course, she'd left it in the house.

But then the noise of the generator hummed to life, and the house lit up from the inside. He went to stand up from his perch, and a gunshot rang through the air.

Avery let out a scream, and Seth jerked before stumbling forward.

A sharp stab of pain pierced Seth's arm the moment he went to stand up. It tore through, and a searing-hot sensation met his muscle. His knees buckled and he dropped to the ground.

He'd gotten the generator to work, and when the noise exploded, he inspected the machine in case it had backfired.

In a swift motion, he put his hand on his arm, willing the pain to subside, and when he removed it, blood covered his palm.

Someone had shot him.

He needed to get to Avery. Where was she?

Seth shifted with his good arm in the wet grass. String lights on the deck illuminated parts of the backyard, and it took his eyes a moment to focus as dizziness swept over him. He refused to pass out. Not when Avery depended on him.

He couldn't allow the same scenario with Logan to play out.

"Seth!" Avery cried out.

She ran over to him, and her quick movements made him nauseous. "Seth. Are you okay? Please tell me you're okay." She bent down next to him, and blood smeared on her hand. Tears streamed down her face. "You're hurt. We need to get to the hospital."

"Hey, it's going to be okay. Shh." He mustered the words despite the pain and offered her a weak smile.

This stung worse than a bullet graze. But he wasn't about to make her panic more.

"I should call an ambulance. But my phone is in the house. Do you have yours?"

As she spoke, the person who shot him came around the corner, a smirk on his face. The guy didn't even have a face covering on, which wasn't a good sign. He was confident enough in his abilities to succeed. Bile rose in his throat.

This man planned to finish the job tonight and not leave anyone to identify him.

"Gun," was all Seth could muster as black dots danced across his vision. He didn't want to guess how much blood he'd lost. Or that the bullet might have hit an artery.

"I know, someone shot you. Stay with me, Seth. Please." Avery cupped his face in her hands.

"I need my gun," he said. The intruder was yards away, and Seth's opportunity to take a shot dwindled.

"Where is it?"

He shifted and let out a grunt.

Everything that followed happened in slow motion—a bad movie playing out in real life. Avery reached across his hip and clamped down on the gun, but Antonio's hit man snagged her arm, weapon pointed between the two of them. She let out a scream and swung around to clobber the guy, but he was too swift. He had a bag over her head in a matter of seconds.

With all his might, Seth pushed himself off the ground, ready to tackle the man. Instead, he was met with a thud as the butt of the gun slammed into his skull.

Avery's muffled scream echoed as the ground came up to meet him and everything went black.

When he came to his senses, cold seeped

through his clothes as wetness clung to his skin. Seth turned on his side and moaned. The pain was still there, and now his head pounded in rhythm with his arm. The motion made him queasy, and he had to lean over as he lost what little he'd eaten recently.

"Avery." He spoke her name, his lips dry. Only silence greeted him. He punched his fist into the ground. They'd taken her.

Sliding his phone out of his pocket, he dialed Grant's number.

"I need backup ASAP." There was no time for greetings. Thankfully his brother understood that.

"You got it," Grant said.

"Can you see my pinned location on your phone? Near the conference center at the cabin."

"Already have it pulled up."

"They took her, and I don't know where they went."

"I'm dispatching officers in that area until I can make it over." Grant typed on the other end.

"Make that an ambulance too, would ya?"

"Why do I have a feeling it's not just for backup in case Avery's hurt?" His brother asked.

"He shot me in the arm," Seth murmured.

"How bad is it?"

"Eh, only a graze."

"You're lying," Grant said.

"Just get backup here fast. The longer it takes, the harder it'll be to find her."

"Don't do anything stupid in the meantime, bro."

A few minutes later, sirens sounded, and Seth walked to the driveway. His steps faltered, as each movement made his head swim.

Two officers climbed out.

"Seth Brown?" asked an older officer with gray speckled hair and glasses.

"Yes, sir." He nodded.

"I'm Lieutenant Walters and this is my partner, Benjamin Kline."

"Thanks for coming so quickly," Seth said, blinking a couple times to erase the blurriness that clouded his eyes.

"You should really sit down. You look like you're about to pass out," Benjamin said as he walked toward him.

"You can have a seat right over here on the truck," a woman medic said as she flagged him down.

"Just a quick patch-up. Then we've got to spread out to find Avery."

The woman took one look at his arm, and he could see wariness invade at his request.

"I'll go to the hospital once I know she's safe."

"Fine." The woman complied and got to work

creating a tight compression around his arm to keep the bleeding at bay.

"What happened?" Walters asked, a pen poised over a pad of paper.

Seth relayed all the information as succinctly as possible.

Walters snapped his notepad shut. "We've got quite a bit of ground to cover here." He turned in a circle.

"You got that right." Trees dotted an endless horizon.

"All right. That should hold for now. Although you really need to see a doctor. It's a nasty graze." The paramedic closed her supply kit.

"Thanks." Seth turned back to the officers. They still had a few hours of daylight left, and the sky had cleared from the storm, which he hoped worked in their favor. "Let's spread out and start looking. He took her toward the tree line." Seth pointed in the direction. "I'll go to the left."

They began to walk, and Seth's feet trudged through the grass like lead. He couldn't give up now. There was too much to lose if he didn't find Avery. And he needed to locate her first. Because he couldn't trust anyone else. Not even the well-meaning officers who'd come to their aid.

Muddy footprints covered the dirt area near

the woods thanks to the rain. Seth wanted to shout for joy. Even in his moment of weakness, he'd been given a glimmer of hope. Something he couldn't take credit for.

He was headed in the right direction.

But right now, there was no sign of Avery.

THIRTEEN

Avery's back ached from the hard surface that pressed into her spine, and her legs had goose bumps from the cold. She tried to focus her eyes on her surroundings, but the area lay shrouded in darkness. Queasiness churned in her stomach, and a headache had formed across her forehead. With a few blinks, she was able to make out the trees around her.

The woods. Seth. Everything came rushing back.

Avery attempted to rub her eyes, but her hands were bound with a zip tie. Panic began to well up inside her. Where was her captor, and why were they still out here?

She needed to come up with a plan, but she didn't know what she was up against.

A twig snapped nearby, and Avery whipped her head around. The sudden motion sent pain ricocheting through her skull.

"Where are you?" a low gravelly voice said. "What do you mean you're stuck?"

Avery shifted against the tree, and she almost let out a groan when her legs refused to move. He'd tied up her feet as well.

"Yeah, I sprayed it, and the stuff knocked her out cold. I've also got her tied up."

She froze, afraid to even breathe, because it might alert this guy to her consciousness.

There had to be a way to escape. Her brain fired in a thousand directions and made it hard to focus. A tear slid down her cheek.

She just had to think. But whatever had been in that bag made her mind fuzzy.

To her left, the guy stood, his back to her. There was a window of time to get away without him noticing. Avery only needed to find a way to get out of these shackles.

It was a good thing whoever was supposed to pick them up had gotten stuck.

Thank You, Lord. Please help me find a way out of this.

In the karate and self-defense courses she'd taken, they practiced situations where someone was tied up. She simply needed to lift her hands high above her head and thrust them down and out.

She glanced to her side to make sure the man still had his gaze averted, then as quietly as possible, she followed through on the motion. Except her muscles were jelly and didn't have their full strength.

C'mon, you can do it.

She pulled her legs in closer, and this time when she spread her hands, the restraint broke and her arms flung out.

Freedom. She'd done it.

"If you don't get here soon, I'm going to kill her myself. Then the rest of the family." The words came out sharp as the man spoke into the phone.

She needed to run, pronto.

Except her legs were bound, and she had to prop her hands on the ground to keep from falling.

The darkness made it harder to see, and her stomach churned.

She was smart. There had to be a way out of this.

She slid her legs in closer and bent forward, unwilling to resign herself to defeat. Not without a fight.

Her eyes squinted against the shadowy forest as she shuffled a few feet and grabbed a twig—the end skinny enough it might work. She wedged it into the opening of the zip tie and pushed it to unlock the mechanism. With a tug, the rubber bond broke loose.

"You've got a minute to get yourself up here or she's a goner. I'm not going to leave her alone to get you out of this mess."

The man's fist connected with a tree trunk.

Avery scrambled to her feet and took off running even though she didn't know which way to go. Anywhere was better than here.

Her legs wobbled, and she tripped over herself, her knee scraping the ground.

"Hey! You're burnt toast, Sanford," the man snarled.

A pit formed in her stomach as she dusted off her hands and pushed forward, forcing her legs to carry her.

The squish squash of feet on the forest floor propelled Avery farther. Tears burned her cheeks, and she blinked several times to focus on what was in front of her.

"Get back here!"

The gnarly voice grew too close for comfort.

She needed someone to know her location. She needed Seth. But he was hurt and needed help too. Which direction was the house in? Sucking air into her diaphragm, she let out a scream at the top of her lungs. "Help!"

A gunshot fired through the air. The bullet whizzed past her and struck the tree bark. Avery's breaths came in pants as she zigzagged her way around the foliage. Black dots danced in her eyes. If she didn't stop for a moment, she would collapse.

Circling around a tree, Avery put her back against the trunk and pulled in air. Silence met her ears. Where was the man? Was he waiting for her to make another move before snatching her?

Several minutes passed before movement to her right caught her attention. A tingling sensation crawled up the base of her neck. The person turned to the side and clutched their arm. A few steps more and their face illuminated in the setting sun.

At the sight of him, Avery's legs nearly buckled. "Seth." She spoke as loudly as she dared, praying he heard her.

Picking up a stone, she threw it as hard as she could, and it hit a tree before landing on the ground. He swiveled around.

"Avery. You're alive."

He closed the gap between them and embraced her in a half hug but grunted at the contact.

"Your arm."

He shook his head. "You're safe, that's all that matters."

The sky peeked through the canopy of leaves. Darkness continued its descent. "Come on, let's get out of here," she said to Seth, mindful to lean on his good arm.

An hour later they sat in the hospital waiting for Seth's X-ray results.

Bags protruded under his eyes, his features etched with pain and weariness.

A knock sounded on the door before an officer made his way into the room. He nodded at Seth before taking a seat in the empty chair adjacent to Avery. "I'm Lieutenant Walters. I presume you're Ms. Sanford?"

"I am," she said. She studied him; his features appeared familiar from somewhere.

"I'm going to need to take your statement."

"Sure." Avery recounted the events of the evening and the words of her captor.

"I'll make sure a BOLO gets out, ASAP," Walters said as he jotted down notes. "That guy's nasty."

Avery stilled. Why did this man presume the identity of the person? Goose bumps dotted her skin, and she turned to look at Seth. Although he appeared unfazed by the officer's comment. Maybe the pain meds had too much of a calming effect, or she was overthinking.

"I'm sorry, do you know the person I described?" Her eyes narrowed as she studied him and slid her chair a few inches back.

"There's been a couple break-ins lately targeting unoccupied homes. A few turned hostile when the owners arrived back too soon."

"I didn't realize it was prominent in the area." Avery leaned back in the chair and relaxed. He was doing his job and didn't have all the facts about her case.

"It doesn't matter whether it's a small town or big city," he said, and slid his glasses on top of his head. "That's all I need for now." Walters gathered his belongings.

"Thanks for your help." Avery shook his hand.

"Certainly. If you need anything else, don't hesitate to reach out." Walters's radio crackled to life, and he shut the door behind him.

"How long until these tests come back?" Seth shifted in the bed. "We need to get a move on. I almost got you killed tonight." His voice caught.

Before she could respond, Seth's phone rang.

"Could you get that for me?" he asked.

Grant's number lit up the screen. "Hey, Grant, it's Avery. You're on speaker."

"Good. Are you both sitting down for this?"

"We are now," Avery said, sliding the chair closer to Seth's side.

"I just got news that Chelsea isn't dead."

The color in Avery's face drained. "Do you know where she's at?" Seth asked as he pushed himself up in the bed, the sheets getting stuck momentarily on his IV.

"No. They only got this tip from a bystander who'd witness the crash and saw a woman matching Chelsea's description standing on the edge of the bank before getting in a car with two men."

"They have her and are torturing her, unless they've killed her already." Avery squeezed her eyes shut.

"But she was under protection," Seth said. Confusion clouded his mind. Whatever the nurse dripped in his IV made it hard to think, even though the pain seemed more bearable at the moment.

Avery stood up. "This doesn't make sense. She wouldn't have just walked into a trap set by these men and given up without a fight. They made sure she'd regret the decision if she walked away and out of their life."

"What if…" Grant stopped.

Did his brother even want to go there? "That's going to be a hefty claim to make, bro," Seth said.

"I know, but we need to start thinking outside the box. Somehow these guys keep finding Avery, and it didn't stop them from locating Chelsea."

"What are you saying?" Avery narrowed her eyes.

Seth let out a sigh. "What if there's someone on the inside working for them?"

"Like a dirty marshal," Grant said. "I've seen it a time or two, sadly."

"It wouldn't make sense." Avery shook her head. "Marcus told me Chelsea opted out of protected services."

Seth raised up onto his good elbow, and the needle in his other arm tugged. This was ridiculous. He needed to get out of the hospital stat. The itch to see justice served and put whoever was involved in this scheme behind bars crawled up his spine. Betrayal by someone who claimed to work on the right side of the law while foiling the truth seared worse than the bullet that had torn through his flesh. But if Chelsea wasn't even in protective custody, they were missing an imperative piece still.

"This isn't adding up." Avery rubbed her hands down her face.

"Don't trust anyone and stay close to Seth." Grant steeled his tone.

"I've got to warn my parents."

"What if that's what they want you to do?" Seth said.

"Regardless of who's working for Antonio, we need to change our approach." Avery rubbed her brow. "We have a house out by Crystal Lake. It was an inheritance from my uncle when he passed away last year. Except for the lawyer, no one else knows about it."

"I think that's a good option." Grant affirmed. "If there's an attack, we'll know who it is."

"Meet us at the lake house for backup, Grant." Seth wasn't about to give his brother a choice. He'd failed Avery too many times and wasn't in a condition to protect her. Not with a bum arm and ear to start off the list.

"Copy that," Grant said and disconnected.

"I'm ready to get out of here." Seth huffed. "I'm tired of feeling incapacitated."

"Yeah, well, you won't be for long." She reached over his side and pressed the red call button.

The feistiness of this woman dug under his skin.

"And for the record, your shortcomings might show where you're weak, but it's a way for God's strength to shine through."

Her words were more healing than the medicine dripping in his IV. Amidst all his failures, she trusted him. Could he trust God and rely on His strength?

She saw something in him that he had a hard time seeing himself. If she trusted him with her life, he would stand by her until these men were caught. Unless. No, he wasn't going to think about the other possibility. Avery was confident in her abilities, so it was time to start relying on the ones God gave him.

"Aye, aye, Captain," he said with a salute. The genuine smile that formed on her face erased all the stress of the situation for a brief moment.

A knock sounded on the door, and a nurse walked into the room. "Do you need something?" She peered at the monitors by the bed.

"Yes, my discharge papers," he said. He caught a sparkle in Avery's eye, which fueled him even more to believe he could actually be the man she needed.

"I see," the nurse said. "The doctor is reviewing your X-ray results and will be in shortly to discuss his findings."

"The sooner he could do so, the better." Seth didn't want to sound impatient, but the clock was ticking.

"I'll let him know," the nurse said and exited.

"I'm going to see if I can find my parents' new numbers and fill them in," Avery said.

Seth was tired of being one step behind these guys and wanted to see the playing field switched. His mind ran through all the leads they had so far on this case. Antonio called the shots somehow from his jail cell, which meant he'd received information from the outside. As well as a list of hit men who could carry out his requests. They'd already identified one dead guy, but Dominic remained elusive, and now they held Chelsea captive somewhere.

Seth groaned. Too many people and moving parts were involved. Taking these people out was much easier said than done.

He grabbed his phone from the portable table at his side and typed a message for Grant.

Has our guy from the diner talked at all?

The response came almost immediately.

Nope. He lawyered up and hasn't said a word.

"How're you feeling?" A voice startled him, and he looked up to see the doctor peering at his papers.

Seth hadn't even heard him walk in. "Ready to get out of this place."

The man chuckled. "Well, you're incredibly fortunate to have only minor damage. The bullet made a clean swipe through the outer part of your arm. After some stitches and a few weeks of PT, you should be fine. Let me get everything I need to stitch you up, then you'll be on your way."

"Great, thank you."

An hour later, Avery wheeled Seth out to their waiting car that Grant dropped off.

"I don't want any more scares like that, got

it?" Avery gave him a solemn expression as she climbed into the driver's seat.

"That goes for you too," he said.

"Deal. Now let's get one step ahead of these goons." Avery smiled and peeled out of the parking lot.

He held back a laugh. He liked her determination, and for once, they were on the same wavelength. "I'd expect nothing less."

Seth just hoped Avery's parents didn't get stuck in the cross fire with their new plan.

FOURTEEN

In a few short hours, Avery would see her parents again, and this mess could be put behind them for good. Surely whoever was leaking information would be discovered and they'd be taken into custody.

"How did your parents take the news?" Seth asked.

Avery kept her eyes on the road. "They weren't thrilled with the idea of relocating for the time being again, but the marshals okayed it, and everyone's on their way to the lake."

"They really don't like the wrench this threw in their life plans, do they?" Seth asked.

"Not one iota." Avery let out a humorless laugh. "Plus, my dad's a cop. He knows how to take care of himself. And he doesn't like the idea of roles being reversed."

"Hmm. Seems like someone else I know." Seth nudged her arm, and Avery gave him a sideways glance.

"Ha. Very funny. If there's one thing the Thompsons excel at, it's not letting anyone step all over us." She missed Logan. They had their fair share of fights and bickering matches. But that's because they were both similar with their strong-willed personalities. Except Logan always came to someone's defense and kept others in their place.

She snuck a glance at Seth, the solemn expression on his face heartbreaking.

"I miss him." He choked on the words, and it almost sent Avery into tears.

"Me too." Being around Seth gave her a glimmer of what life used to be like with Logan. Before his deployment.

"You remind me a lot of him. In good ways," Seth said. He took her hand in his and caressed her palm.

"Thanks," she said. The tenderness of his heart amazed her. The ways he cared and wanted the best for those around him. A sense of guilt invaded her as she remembered the accusations she'd harbored in her heart against him. "I'm sorry for blaming you for Logan's death."

His hand stilled. "You didn't know the whole story."

"But I should have believed the best about you and everyone involved."

"Sometimes that naivete can prove dangerous."

Like right now. Trying to take a gamble at who could be trusted. And the only way to see someone's true colors was over time with their actions. Except that didn't give them a lot of leverage in the current situation.

Avery let out a sigh.

Her phone announced an incoming call.

"Hi, Mom, you're on speaker," she said as the call connected to Bluetooth.

"We're almost to the lake house, but I left my sparkly knitting needles at the house." She rattled off the new address, and Seth jotted it down. "I think they're on the coffee table, because they're not in my bag. I was working on my project last night."

"And in the scramble, I left my file that has extra notes in the office. It should be labeled Freedom," her dad chimed in. "Could you swing by and grab them before you meet us?"

"Not a problem. We'll take the detour and collect what you need and see you soon."

"Sparkly knitting needles?" Seth asked, his eyebrows raised.

"She claims it's her secret weapon to a successful piece of clothing. And most of those pieces are already in a select wardrobe for her future grandkids."

"Is that anywhere on the horizon?" Seth asked.

Avery swallowed; her mouth was dry as she

tried to formulate a response without thinking too deeply about Seth's question. "Not anytime soon. And you?" Avery bit her lip. Why did she insist on continuing an already awkward conversation?

"Negative," he said.

So that confirmed her suspicion about his singleness.

"Was there anyone at one time?" Seth asked, his voice deep.

"Yeah, but it didn't last when he wanted a stay-at-home wife who'd host all his ritzy friends. I wanted to do things with my life, not have my independence squandered."

"Ouch. That sounds stuffy."

"You don't say," Avery exclaimed. "What about you?"

"I was engaged once."

Avery's hand went slack on the steering wheel. That was not the response she anticipated. "What happened?"

"When I was discharged from the Army, my physical limitations didn't meet her standards, and she ran off with another guy."

"Seth, I'm so sorry."

"Don't be. It was for the best."

The safe house her parents had stayed at came into view, and the conversation shifted.

"If you could look for my mom's needles, I'll

find the office and grab my dad's papers," she said as they walked up the front path. Her eyes scanned the surroundings, her mind in constant fight-or-flight response.

She punched in the security code her mom gave her to get into the house, and they split off. Avery passed by a coat closet and made her way upstairs, opening doors until she found the office and let out a whistle.

Her dad had clearly stayed busy with work, unable to put those sleuthing skills to rest. Papers lay across every square inch of the room and covered the desk, floor and wall. A whiteboard hung in the corner with sticky notes and marker scribbles.

It was going to take a moment to find the folder he'd requested. She began to rummage through the papers in the file organizer, each one marked on the outside with a label.

Not being successful there, she began sifting through the stack on his desk. A robbery and kidnapping cold cases took up a binder.

A knock sounded on the door, and Avery jumped.

"Sorry. I was trying to avoid that," Seth said.

Avery turned around, her hand on her chest.

"Find what you were looking for?"

"Not yet. There's more here than I was expecting." Avery waved her hand around the space.

Seth stepped in and surveyed the area. "You're not kidding." He walked over to the whiteboard and planted his hands on his hips. "Looks like he's been busy trying to nail the cartel."

Avery placed the papers back on the desk and made her way over to him. "Yeah, it was in his jurisdiction until he went into WITSEC. That's Antonio. And Dominic," she said, pointing to a mug shot and a picture of the two men in an alleyway shaking hands. The tattoos on their arms gave away their gang affiliation.

A few email correspondences were pinned up with a magnet.

We need to figure out who the third leader is, or this ring won't be busted.

They're too good at covering their tracks, and my leads have gotten me nowhere.

Run these pictures through the system, and see if anything comes back as a hit. I know it's a long shot, but it's worth a try if it means getting back to normalcy.

Three pictures hung next to the emails and had red circles around someone. The person was blurry based on the side angle position in each image, but they had their hair in a topknot. Although it could have easily been a man bun or a women's hairstyle.

"Look at this." Avery pointed to the board. "These emails were between my dad and an unnamed recipient. Except there's no reply on what he found with the images."

"What's the time stamp?"

"About a week or so before my parents went into the program."

"Do you recognize who this is?" Seth indicated the individual circled in red.

"I wish, but it's too hard from the side profile to make out." She let out a sigh. They needed some kind of breakthrough soon.

"We can see if your dad has any other ideas."

"You're right," she said as she snapped a few pictures of the board to show her dad later.

A door slammed below them. Avery stilled even as her hands shook.

"Are you expecting anyone?" Seth asked as he backed up closer to the office door.

She shook her head and followed him. "Unless it's the marshals?" The question came out in a squeak.

"I guess there's only one way to find out," Seth said, his hand on the door.

Seth inched closer to the only point of entry and exit in the room. He sincerely hoped it was the marshals or her parents, but his gut told him not to hold his breath. There were no trackers that he'd seen when making his rounds, and they hadn't been followed.

Which only confirmed their suspicion about someone on the inside feeding information to the cartel.

Waves of nausea churned in his stomach. How could anyone betray their fellow brother or sister like that?

Seth turned with his good ear up against the door and listened. Silence echoed back.

The notes Avery's dad had on this case confirmed the intricacy of it all. And if Seth didn't keep Avery safe, not only would justice fail to be served, but he'd never forgive himself for letting Avery down.

He leaned forward and pulled a gun from his ankle holster and handed it to Avery before reaching across his lower back and extracting a second weapon for himself. Her eyes widened as she took the gun from him and weighed it in her hands.

"Have you ever shot one before?" he asked.

She swallowed hard. "A few times given my dad's a cop."

"Good." He'd figured that would be her response because now wasn't the best time to give someone a crash course. "Keep it close."

He debated telling her to stay here while he investigated, but decided against it.

With a featherlight grip on the handle, he opened the door, hoping the hinges wouldn't squeak. He scanned the hallway before taking a few steps out toward the staircase, Avery covering his back.

They descended a couple of steps before a voice stopped him in his tracks.

"Yes. I'm here."

That voice rang a bell, but his mind came up empty on a face.

He raised an eyebrow to convey his question to her. Who was here? And how'd they know where Avery's parents lived?

Avery must have read his mind, because she shrugged her shoulders.

Seth took another step, but the smell of gasoline wafted through the air and tickled his nostrils. "Do you smell that?" he whispered.

"Yeah," she grimaced.

"Yes, yes. I know. The evidence will be destroyed soon," the person said.

Avery gasped.

They were going to burn the house down.

Seth figured the person talked to someone on the phone, as he didn't hear any other voices.

Questions riddled his mind, and Seth wanted

answers. He wouldn't let someone get away with this.

The person let out a groan. "Fine. I'll get the papers so you can dispose of them yourself and send proof that the rest of the house was taken care of."

Footsteps headed their way, and Avery's hand squeezed his bicep, her grip tight with desperation. "What do we do?" she asked.

There was no time to think through an extensive plan with multiple options like his training days had taught him. No. Instead, he needed to find a way to stop this person in his tracks with minimal damage.

Before he could voice anything, Avery said, "We've got to grab those photos. And notes."

"I'll distract them while you collect as much of it as you can. See if they'll talk at all." He could see the skepticism in her features, but their options at the moment were limited.

"Please be careful," she said, then made her way back to the office.

Seth snapped his weapon back into its holder so as not to alarm the intruder. Once on the main floor, he listened for which direction the man's footsteps came from and rounded the corner.

His heart thundered in his chest as he came face-to-face with one of the men responsible for the hit on Avery's life—multiple times for that matter.

"Officer Walters." Seth kept his tone even and smiled despite the anger and confusion that brewed. The realization that a dirty cop had been sitting in their presence mere hours ago knocked the breath from him.

The look on the man's face paled, and his eyes widened. "Mr. Brown. You scared me. I didn't think anyone was here."

"I heard someone come in, but I was busy finding these for Avery." He held up the pink-and-gray knitting needles; the sparkles glinted from the sunlight that streamed through the window. "I was told these are a necessity for her projects." He let out a chuckle.

"Ah, yes. Some women sure love their hobbies." He paused and peered past Seth's shoulder. "Is Avery here too?"

"I said I'd run the errand for her." He wasn't about to disclose her location. Not until the man exposed his intentions. "Did someone send you here for something as well?"

"A call came in about a prowler on the premise, and I came to check it out." Walters took a few steps back to create distance between them.

Did Walters think he could fool them? The smell of gasoline strengthened down here, not something that could go unnoticed or unquestioned.

There was no way Seth was letting Walters near Avery either.

"Actually, since you're here, you could help me investigate the gas smell. I got here and was concerned there might be a leak somewhere since it's so strong. Do you know where the furnace is located?" Seth asked. He waited to see if Walters would take the bait.

The officer turned his wrist to look at his watch. "I guess I have a few extra minutes. Sure."

What Seth really wanted to do was demand answers. Like how he found the house where Avery's parents lived.

"Is there a gas stove in the kitchen?"

"Over there." Walters pointed past the dining room.

Seth eyed the man as he stood by the appliance and listened for any kind of whistle or hissing sound. After several seconds ticked by and satisfied that he showed enough concern here for the story to be believable, he stepped away.

"Maybe it's the water heater," Seth said. "Although I should call the fire department just to be safe." He reached for his phone and opened up the basement door.

"No." Walters's voice rose. "I mean, I really don't think there's a need."

"Why not?" Seth narrowed his gaze.

"Why are you asking so many questions?"

Seth could see the jitters and skittishness in the cop's eyes.

"I think if we just—" Before he had time to finish his sentence, Walters rounded on him and swung. The action caught Seth off guard, and he missed the chance to intercept. Instead, the punch landed square against his jaw, and pain ricocheted through his molars. He stumbled back and grabbed the handrail.

Walters pulled his gun as Seth reached for his.

"Put your weapon down." Walters commanded.

Seth had a clear shot at the man. He wouldn't back down now. "No." He lifted his gun high just as a shot rang out.

Seth ducked and returned fire.

The bullet chipped off wood as the door slammed shut. Seth tried the knob, but Walters had already barricaded it somehow. He needed to bust down the door. Only seconds remained before gasoline and flames would engulf the air around him.

FIFTEEN

Avery shoved another folder in her purse and froze at the sound of Walters's voice. Fire burned in her veins at the men's conversation.

Footsteps pounded up the stairs. She was trapped. Avery looked at the office, wishing there was a window or some way to escape.

The cool metal comforted her as she gripped the gun in her hand tighter. She could defend herself. Seth believed in her; she'd seen it in his eyes when he'd given her the weapon and the way he'd let her cover his back. Warmth flooded her arms. Yes, she was grateful to have him at her side—even though the circumstances were less than fitting.

Her ears began to ring as she strained to listen for movement on the other side of the door.

These men would not win. Too much had already been taken.

Not hearing anything, she opened the door,

gun pointed as she swiveled on her heel in a one-eighty.

"I suggest you drop the weapon."

Avery whipped around to see Walters standing a few feet away, his own gun drawn.

"Where's Seth?" she asked through clenched teeth.

"I said put the gun down."

The dark center of his barrel aimed at her chest. He wasn't joking around. Avery crouched down and placed the Glock on the floor, keeping her hands visible.

"Kick it over here."

She did what she was told.

There had to be a way to stall him. Figure out how to distract and get close enough to incapacitate him with a good old lunge punch. Of course, right now that tactic wouldn't work.

Forgive me, Lord. I've been trusting my own strength instead of You. Show me what to do to make it out of here alive. I want to walk in faith that Your rod and staff comfort me.

Whatever the outcome, God would protect her.

And help me find Seth. Please let him be okay.

She uttered the prayer and focused on her breathing. If she panicked, anything she attempted would be futile.

"How could you do this?" she asked, not exactly referencing a specific incident but hoping he would divulge information.

"Get back in the room." He tilted his head to the left.

Avery inched back. "How did you know where my parents lived? Who are you working for?"

"It wasn't that hard," he said, his tone flat. "I stuck a listening and tracking device on your purse back at the hospital. Then you did the rest of the work."

"I... I don't understand." Avery's hands shook.

"Every cop needs to be resourceful. That's how we help people."

His reasoning sounded illogical, but she couldn't say that while he pointed a gun at her.

Walters stepped forward, and Avery moved to the side.

"Were you the one who had the email correspondence with my dad?"

"We worked several cases together over the years."

A pit formed in Avery's stomach. "My dad trusted you, and you betrayed him." She spat the words.

"I didn't have a choice." A flicker of emotion creased his forehead.

"There's always a choice to make. We're responsible for our actions."

"You don't know the whole story." He stared her down.

"Maybe I can help." She spoke the words softly, changing tactics.

"Enough!" his voice boomed. "Get back in the office." He waved the gun toward the room, his finger hovering too close for comfort on the trigger.

"Where's Chelsea? What did they do to her?"

"I don't ask questions. Simply follow orders."

She inched her way back into the space. "If you're planning to kill me, it might be good to provide a confession first."

"I'm sorry. I really wish it didn't have to come to this." He pulled out a pair of handcuffs and clipped one side to the back of the chair. "Sit down."

The muzzle suctioned against her temple, and she wanted to cry but refused to give him the satisfaction. If she tried any defense moves, she'd be dead in a second. The click of the metal secured her imprisonment and any chance of escape. And soon there'd be little opportunity for answers.

"Someone will come looking for me, you know."

"Not when this place is charred and your parents find out the cartel got to you first."

Avery jerked against the seat. "You wouldn't dare. You took a pledge to defend life and justice, not destroy it."

Walters clenched his fist and rubbed his graying hair. "There was no other way. You don't understand!"

"Try me." She stared him in the eye, refusing to think about the gun still held against her temple.

"There's no time. He'll show up any minute."

And with that, he backed out of the room and shut the door.

"Seth!" she screamed. "Help. Anyone!"

A tear trailed down her cheek, but she couldn't even wipe it away. Out of all the ways to die, being burned alive was not one she wanted to experience.

She looked around the room, willing something, anything, to appear that she could use to break free of the cuffs. Perhaps her dad had keys in his drawer to pick the lock. With an awkward hop and slide motion, Avery positioned herself in front of the desk and used her foot to open each drawer. More files occupied one. A stash of lollipops and chocolate candy sat in another.

The smell of gasoline and smoke filtered through the air. She needed to hurry.

"Seth!" she yelled his name once more, each breath wasted in the enclosed space when no response came.

The top drawer had several knickknacks and office supplies. A few paper clips lay in a pile, and she wanted to shout for joy. Turning herself around, she stood in a squatting position and reached around with her hands until they clamped down on the thin metal.

She fumbled with the clip, trying to unravel it partially so it would fit in the hole. Her finger slipped, and the end pricked her under the nail before it dropped to the floor. A groan escaped. There wasn't time for mistakes.

As she went to grab another one, the office door swung open and hit the wall.

Seth stood there with soot on his face and let out a sigh of relief. "Thank God you're okay." His knees nearly buckled before he shut the door and rushed to her side.

"What happened? He didn't—" Avery choked on the words and stared at him, searching his eyes to make sure he was truly standing here in one piece in front of her.

He cupped her face in his hands and pressed a kiss to her forehead. "I'll tell you later. Now is not the time. There's a blaze going strong downstairs." He let out a cough.

The warmth of his lips impressed on her head like a sealed stamp promising more to come later. Oh, how grateful she was to see him alive. Although now was not the most ideal situation to let her feelings take over. She had lots of questions. Like what he meant by that short peck.

Was it simply the rush of adrenaline? "Can you grab that paper clip? I think we might be able to use it to pick the lock."

In a few minutes, Seth broke open the cuffs, and Avery rubbed her wrists.

"Let's get out of here," he said.

She placed her hand on the door and didn't feel excessive heat, so they scrambled out into the hall but stopped short of the stairs at the sight of ascending flames licking the wood.

A crash sounded down below, and Avery cringed. It was only a matter of time before the second story collapsed.

"We've got to find another way out." Seth looked at her. "How far down is it to jump from here?"

Avery ran into the bathroom to peer out the window. "At least fifteen feet." Which meant the risk of injury was great. But it was worth the gamble if it meant avoiding asphyxiation.

A cough expelled from Seth's lungs, the smoke building. She put her shirt over her mouth and blinked a few times.

"It's that or nothing. We need to move," Seth said as they made their way toward the window.

Sweat beaded on Seth's brow and arms, the warmth in the house rising rapidly.

He'd gotten to Avery's side only to see they'd

need a second miracle as he peered out the window. Because the drop below was steep. Only the front walkway and a few bushes in the yard would halt their fall. Although heights had never bothered him before, a wave of nausea swirled around him as he unlatched the window.

He'd been able to shoot a few rounds to weaken the doorknob where Walters had locked him before kicking out the basement door, and now they'd need to freefall out the second story.

I know I haven't been the best at praying lately. But there's nowhere else to turn, Lord, but You. Help me be brave, God. No matter the outcome. You already helped me past one hurdle. I want to believe You can give me the strength again.

The screen protecting anyone from tumbling over the edge clattered to the ground in a matter of seconds. Seth's mind wrestled with whether to jump first or be chivalrous and let Avery go so she wouldn't be stuck in a burning house a second longer.

Thankfully he didn't have to decide because she broke the silence first. "Wait." She placed a hand on his shoulder and took a step back.

Avery's face appeared a shade paler. Was she having second thoughts? If he had to jump with her in his arms, so be it, because he wasn't about to succumb to the other possibility.

"There isn't time to second-guess." He spoke louder, the roar of the blaze growing.

"I know." She tugged on her hair and put it in a bun. "I just remembered seeing a sliding glass door in the one room I canvassed while locating the office. It could be a balcony. I think it's worth a shot."

"And if not?" Impatience laced his tone.

"Then we jump from that window." Her lips set into a thin line.

Aside from his better judgment, he complied. "Let's hurry."

He lifted his shirt above his nose as they ducked back into the hall. The smoke was thicker and black. A cough racked Avery's frame as she walked low to the ground. He kept his gaze on her feet to keep from getting lost.

The floor under his feet sagged, and he took each step gingerly, so it wouldn't collapse and swallow them whole.

Avery stopped moving, and he waited. Time frozen yet moving at warp speed.

"I don't like how weak this feels." She tapped the floor in front of her with the tip of her toe.

"Let me go first." Seth stepped diagonal to avoid the compromised infrastructure. The floor creaked, and Seth held his breath. When nothing else happened, he extended his hand to Avery, who leapt over to his side.

She grabbed the stairway banister with her other hand to steady herself and let out a yelp. Avery's hand flung back and connected with his knee.

"Sorry," she yelled. "It's scorching."

They stepped into the room, and he slammed the door shut with his elbow. A small reprieve offered them better visibility, but it wouldn't be for long. Smoke already trickled under the door frame.

"Over here. It's here." Avery shouted and waved her arms.

Sure enough, a sliding glass door greeted them and was accompanied by a balcony. The fresh air enveloped Seth's lungs and caused them to burn. He let out a cough and braced his hands on the railing. Bushes and plush grass dotted the backyard below them. Except there were no stairs. "Looks like we're sliding down firefighter style." He pointed to the poles holding up the structure.

"I'm okay with that," Avery said as she swung her leg over the banister.

Careful not to get splinters from the wood, Seth maneuvered down the pole. His feet touched the solid ground, and Avery rushed him with a hug that nearly tackled him to the ground.

"Thank you, Jesus. We're alive," he said into the crevice of her shoulder.

Avery pulled back and looked him in the eye. "My parents. We need to get to the lake house before Walters."

"I'm on it." Seth tugged his phone from his back pocket and dialed Grant's number. Satisfied that an officer would get to the lake house before they did to alert the marshals, he said, "Let's get moving. We need to get the firefighters here ASAP."

"Already on it." Avery held her phone to her ear. She relayed information to the dispatcher as they headed around the corner, farther away from the blaze.

But the sight in front of him made him stop short and grab Avery's arm. "Don't move," he whispered.

Up ahead, Walters stood taking pictures of the house. Seth curled his fist—the audacity of this man. He wouldn't get away with this. Walters shifted slightly to get a better angle of the second story.

"You sneak up behind him, and I'll come in from the side." Seth drew his weapon, prepared for a counter attack.

"Copy that." Avery made a wide circle to avoid Walters direct line of sight.

By the time Walters sensed someone's presence, Avery had him in a choke hold on the ground.

The man writhed in her grasp.

"I wouldn't fight it if I were you. Cops are already on the way." Seth steadied the gun in case he tried anything stupid.

"There's a lot of explaining to do," Avery said.

"I'm sorry, I'm so sorry." Walters's voice cracked and tears glistened in his eyes.

This was not the response Seth expected, and part of him wasn't sure if he should feel sorry for him. The guy could easily be putting on a facade. Make them pity him, and when they lowered their guard, take the upper hand.

"If you start talking, they might let you off easier, considering the consequences are already high for a cop."

"It doesn't matter. When they find out I didn't do my job, I'll no longer be of any need."

"Why'd you do it?" Seth asked, cutting to the chase.

"It's not easy being a cop."

"It's not easy defending your country either. But that's no reason for excuses." Seth ground his teeth. "You had a choice."

"I was in too much pain. I needed relief."

"What do you mean?" Avery asked. Her grip on Walters unchanged.

"I broke my tibia a few years back. Never fully recovered."

Seth raised an eyebrow and looked at Avery, curious about where this story was going.

"And…" he prodded.

"The surgery was expensive. I couldn't afford to miss more time at work. But the pain was unbearable. Eventually my doctor stopped signing off on a prescription."

Guilt tugged at Seth. Here they were listening to this man while the house behind them burned to a crisp. Seth hoped the fire crew would come around the bend any minute. Knowing there was nothing he could do, he tuned back into what Walters was saying.

"They promised to give me drugs to help the pain in exchange for their freedom."

"Who's *they*?" Avery asked warily.

Walters cleared his throat but didn't say anything.

"It's Antonio and Dominic, isn't it?"

"Doesn't matter. All I know is I've done a terrible thing, and there's no backing out."

"You have a chance to make this right," Avery said. A knowing look passed between her and Seth. Affirmation on what she'd helped him see about his own mistakes.

"No." He shook his head. "I'm indebted to them forever. I know too much about their inner workings." He let out a groan.

A car engine roared to life and came down

the drive. The black Cadillac's tinted windows provided obscurity, and Seth doubted it was an unmarked police car given the current situation.

"You need to run now." Walters kinked his head to the side to inspect the car before turning back toward Avery.

"When this could all end right here?" Avery's tone was adamant. "Not a chance."

"You don't understand who you're dealing with," Walters cried.

Seth's gut told him to listen to Walters and flee.

"Please. At least let me do one right thing."

Without waiting for an answer, Seth grabbed Avery's wrist and pulled her off Walters.

"What are you doing? He's going to get away," she protested in his grasp.

"Don't make me pick you up." He steeled his gaze on hers and tugged once more. The car pulled into the drive and parked.

"Go," Walters begged.

With Avery's hand in his, they took off in a sprint toward the back of the house. A car door slammed shut, and Seth winced. A voice shouted, but he couldn't make out what was being said.

Sirens pierced the air. A gunshot rang out and more rounds followed. There had to be a way to get a glance at who hid in the vehicle.

SIXTEEN

All Avery wanted was to turn around and watch Walters and whoever was in that Cadillac get read their Miranda rights and hauled away. The satisfaction of knowing they were off the streets burned in her chest. Or maybe that was simply smoke inhalation.

Either way, there was no opportunity to be a spectator as Seth's firm grasp on her hand pulled her to their waiting car. Heat crept into her cheeks and coursed through her arm from the security of being in his hold.

Seth opened the driver's side and ushered her in.

"What are you doing?" She stared up into his dark chocolaty eyes. He towered over her with his hands propped on the roof. His figure shouted a confidence he'd lacked before. His eyes glinted with determination.

"If anyone comes over this way, hightail it out

of here." He tossed her the keys. "I'm going to see if I can get a good look at who's in the Cadillac. We need evidence."

"But…" Avery protested.

Seth put his finger on her lips. "Do you trust me?"

There was that word again: trust.

Avery let out a groan. It would be so much easier if she knew how all this would end. But that would defeat the purpose of trusting God. The truth seeped into her mind as the Lord gently reminded her of what wouldn't change. Regardless of the outcome, the Lord was with her now, and he would be for eternity. Even though she was walking through the valley of the shadow of death.

"I've been trained for this kind of work."

How would he know where to find her if she had to escape?

As if on cue, he said, "I'll find you." He pressed a kiss to her cheek and winked.

Seth headed back toward the property and disappeared around a bush. Smoke continued to rise in gray billows from the house.

Avery slid the key into the ignition, prepared to start the engine on a second's notice. Then she grabbed her purse and yanked out the listening and tracking device Walters had planted. No one else would get the satisfaction of spying on her. She dug her heel into the dirt by the car until the bug resembled hundreds of shattered pieces.

Minutes later, Seth jogged back and signaled for her to start the car. He hopped in, and she maneuvered her way back to the main road.

"Anything?"

"Negative." He frowned. "Whoever it was got away. So we need to get to your parents before Antonio's clan."

Avery pressed down on the gas harder and gripped the steering wheel. A stinging sensation ignited on her palm. "Ow." She lifted her hand to see blisters bubbling on the surface, the skin red and peeling.

"That's a nasty burn," Seth said as he inspected the area. "That needs some serious attention."

"It'll have to wait."

"I can't bear the thought of something happening to you." He pulled in a breath. "I care about you."

Yes, she could second that statement. The more time she spent with him, the harder it seemed to imagine life without him in it. "Something we should discuss when all this is over." It took everything in her to focus on the road and not pull over and kiss him.

"Agreed." The smoothness of Seth's lips

brushed against her skin as he planted a feather-light kiss on her hand.

"Do you have the papers?"

"Right there." Avery pointed to her purse, grateful they hadn't burned with the rest of the property.

An hour later, the lake house came into view, and memories of childhood summers at her uncle's estate danced around. Carrying around hunks of watermelon before discarding the rinds and catapulting off the dock into the water. Catching frogs and staying up past her bedtime for campfires.

As she stepped out of the car, Avery caught a glimpse of herself in the mirror. Her hair frizzed in all directions, and her features darkened from smoke and ash. She braced herself for the bombardment of questions and explaining her parents would expect. Nothing appeared amiss from the picture-perfect view. Avery hoped they finally got ahead of Antonio's plan.

"Do you have the knitting needles?" she asked, and smiled when Seth flaunted them in the air.

With a knock, she opened the door and stepped inside. "We come bearing gifts," she proclaimed.

Her own voice echoed in greeting. "Mom, Dad?" She gave Seth a quizzical look. "Where are the marshals? There should be two here at least."

"Maybe they're outside? Catching some rays on the lake?" He lifted his brow.

She walked into the living room and let out a gasp. Cushions were overturned, pictures lay strewn on the floor, and knickknacks littered the place.

"Is everything okay? Mom? Dad?" she called out once more.

A shoe caught her attention by the side of the couch. She rounded the corner, and her hands flew to her mouth. One of the marshals lay sprawled on the ground.

"Call 911. We've got a marshal down." Avery turned to Seth.

He raced to where she crouched and put his fingers on the man's neck. "Got a pulse. But he's knocked out cold."

They stood, and Avery quickened her pace to the kitchen. The sight in front of her sent her grasping for the counter so she wouldn't collapse. Broken glass and shards of dishes created an unwanted mosaic on the tile floor, the counter wet with soapy water.

Drops of blood trailed from the sink and trickled down the wood cabinets, and all Avery could see was her mom or dad injured somewhere.

"They took them. They got here first." Avery raced out the back door down to the dock area. Her eyes flitted around, looking for any signs of movement.

She cupped her hands and yelled their names again. Only the birds chirped in response.

"Didn't Grant send an officer over here?" Avery asked Seth. She'd sensed his presence there before he even spoke a word.

"He did. So either he got tied up elsewhere, or he's here but unable to respond."

An uneasy feeling settled in her stomach. Too many people were hurt at her expense. She couldn't afford to add any more to the list.

They combed the area, searching for any indication of someone or signs of a struggle and found the other marshal by the shrubbery near the patio. Seth grasped the man's wrist. "He's alive but drugged too."

Avery's shoulders slumped. Who would be found injured next?

She helped Seth lift the marshal and move him into the air-conditioned house. Her hand throbbed as the cloth fabric brushed against the open flesh wound when she set the guy down.

"We're going to find them," Seth said.

As if on cue, the phone in the kitchen rang. The noise caused both of them to jump.

She furrowed her brow before picking it up.

"Hello?" Static greeted her on the other end.

"Hello?" she said again.

"If you want to see your parents again, I suggest you listen closely."

"Who is this?" Avery lifted the phone away from her ear to check caller ID. Except it showed a blocked number. The person's voice was distorted and made it impossible to know who was speaking. "You're such a coward to hide like this."

The person laughed. "You think you have this all figured out, Avery Sanford. But let me assure you, you never will." Whoever spoke lowered their voice.

"What do you want?"

"The pictures and correspondence. All the evidence."

"How do we get it to you?" Avery asked.

"Be quiet! Nine tonight. At the cabin off North Shore Road." Avery waved Seth over, indicating she needed a pen and paper. He whipped out his phone, pulled open a new note and handed it to her. She typed the directions.

"How do I know my parents are there?"

A grunt sounded in the background, and her mom shouted something.

New tears sprung to her eyes, and she squeezed them shut.

"No cops. And especially not that military hunk of a boyfriend," the person snapped.

Before Avery could respond, the line went dead.

Seth only heard Avery's side of the conversation, but whatever had been conveyed wasn't good given the tremor in her fingers. They should have been one step ahead by coming to this undisclosed location.

Except these masterminds still called the shots. Which meant this might not end in their favor. And those he tried to protect could get hurt once more. He curled his fist. The urge to knock these guys out and shatter the stark reality of evil winning was strong.

The temptation to bombard Avery with questions sat at the forefront of his mind, but it wouldn't be helpful. He couldn't change anything to make it better.

What if there was another dirty officer working with the marshals? The uncertainty of it all made his mind spin.

"We're going to find them," he said. "At least we have an address." He pointed to his phone. "That's progress."

"But the moment I hand the papers over, it's done." She let out a sigh.

"Were you able to decipher who was talking?" There had to be clues somewhere. Something that would pin these people down and put them behind bars for good.

"No. They distorted their voice."

"Well, if that's the game they want to play, we'll match it with our own forces."

"They said no cops." Avery sat down at the kitchen table. "And I believe them. They'll kill my parents before we step one foot onto the premises."

Avery was scared for her parents' safety. He could see it in her eyes. But there had to be a plan that prioritized her safety and allowed backup to get in too.

"Were there any other stipulations?" he asked.

"Nine tonight. The evidence with me and no cops or…" Avery gave him a once-over. "That military hunk of a boyfriend," she finished.

"Boyfriend, huh?" Seth smirked.

"You know it has a nice sound to it." Avery leaned her head to the side and smiled.

"I'm glad you think so." Seth enveloped her in a hug, and the sound of his heartbeat brought a rhythm of normalcy.

"First, we need to focus." Avery stepped back.

"We could get Grant to wire us up and be ready with a team."

His phone buzzed with a message from his brother.

"Grant and Loki just pulled up."

He sent back a reply for them to come in, and a few seconds later, Loki barreled through the hall to their side. It was as if the dog sensed something was wrong, and sidled up to Avery, nudging her nose along her leg.

"I've got some news to fill you in on." His brother's face was grim as he pulled up a chair and sat. Grant seemed to notice something else was amiss, because he shifted his gaze between Seth and Avery.

"They're gone. Someone got here before your officer and took them," Seth said.

"How?" Grant furrowed his brow.

"Walters had a listening device on when he came to the hospital for our statements." Avery frowned.

"Well, he won't be able to testify to that."

"He escaped, didn't he?" Avery asked, and Seth bit his tongue, knowing it was far more sinister from the glimpse he'd gotten behind the shrubs earlier.

"He was killed. Shot execution style."

Seth closed his eyes and sadness filled him at the loss of life. Yet, he lifted up a short prayer of thanks for his and Avery's safety.

"He died doing a noble thing," Seth said. "He made sure we got away and wouldn't endure the same fate." There'd been too many close calls for Seth's comfort. "Did you get the plates on the Cadillac?"

"Yeah, but it's a dead end," Grant said.

"Let me guess, the plates came back as a stolen vehicle."

"Bingo." Grant snapped his fingers.

"And the officer coming to watch my parents?" Avery asked as she rubbed Loki's head. "Is he okay?"

"He'll be fine. I got a call from him that someone ran him off the road, and he was stuck in a ditch. More annoyed than anything. The only scratches were to the vehicle."

"And the house?" she asked.

"Firefighters were still battling the blaze when I left to come here. Unfortunately, it doesn't look promising."

"We need to come up with a game plan," Seth said. "Where are the files you grabbed?" he asked Avery.

"Here." She pulled them out of the bag and set them on the table.

"There's one more thing you should know," Grant interjected.

"I don't like the sound of that," Seth said watching his brother.

"The other guy we took into custody from the diner was found dead in his holding cell early this morning."

"One more lead severed." Seth growled.

"I want to get my parents back," Avery said, slapping her hand on the table.

While Grant collected samples of blood and dusted for fingerprints, Seth scoured the papers and pictures once more, looking for anything they missed previously that would nail this once and for all.

"Look at this." Avery slid a paper his way.

"We know Antonio is the head of this ring, and Dominic is an elite in his chain of command. And Thunder Cloud is the name Antonio goes by." Seth sifted through all the information they did know. Speaking it out loud helped his brain process it.

"Exactly." Avery nodded. "And we're trying to figure out who the third person in these other photos are that my dad had."

Seth skimmed over the conversation again. "Who your dad believes is someone who goes by Fireball."

"Right. And he indicated he knew their real name and that this whole operation was about to be exposed." Avery pointed to the last line at the bottom of the dialogue.

Avery flipped through another paper and let out a hiss before waving her hand in the air. "Paper cut." She grimaced.

"Why don't you go wash your hand then wrap

it up along with those blisters so they don't get infected?"

"Okay. There should be a first-aid kit under the sink," she said and headed down the hall.

"Can you run the alias Fireball through the database and see if it generates any leads?" Seth asked Grant, who was cleaning up his supplies.

"Sure thing. These people think they are high and mighty with their fierce titles."

"You can say that again." Seth rummaged around and finally found the bandages stowed in a cabinet above the microwave.

"I'm going to make a few phone calls. Then I have an idea for a takedown tonight."

Seth was thankful to have his brother's support, even though there were a million other things on his to-do list.

Another several minutes ticked by, and Avery still wasn't out of the bathroom yet. What was taking her so long? He walked down the hall, peering in each room, until he found a closed door, hoping it was the right one.

He knocked. "I promise it's not going to hurt as bad as bandaging your side," he said, keeping his tone light.

When there was no response, Seth toggled the knob and opened the door.

"Avery, you okay?" He peered in, but the bathroom was empty.

He swiveled on his heel and headed back to the main area only to hear a car engine spur to life.

His darn ear. Somehow, she'd snuck out without him hearing.

Seth stepped onto the porch as Avery buckled her seat belt.

He barreled down the drive to intercept the vehicle. His hand slammed on the hood. The metal scorched his skin from its direct position in the sunlight. He glided it along the surface, afraid to let go because she might drive off without him.

With a quick sweep to open the door, he slid inside and turned toward her with a tap on the dash. "Let's go."

Seth wasn't about to let her encounter this threat alone.

Tonight, the tides would turn, for the good.

Even though it meant putting his life on the line to meet the person who wanted her dead.

SEVENTEEN

"You're going to get us both killed!" Avery cried.

"There's no way I'm leaving you alone to do this." Seth planted his feet on the floorboard and buckled up.

Avery let out a huff. The voice on the phone elevated her fears. "They said you couldn't come." Not if she wanted to see her parents alive.

Seth crossed his arms. "I'm not going down without a fight, and I doubt you are either."

He focused straight ahead, his jaw clenched. Something shifted in his disposition. "What's changed?" she asked.

"I made a promise to keep you safe. Because I care about you. And for Logan's sake. If there's one thing I'm learning, it's to keep fighting regardless of the odds stacked up. Even when I don't have the strength."

"Who showed you that?" Avery squinted against the sun now low in the sky.

"God."

"How so?"

"Through you," he whispered. His gaze fixed on her, and it made her light-headed.

Was she willing to trust this man with her life? Avery pulled out of the driveway. "We've got some people to save." She drove one handed, the pain in her other hand made it difficult to even move her fingers. She really should have bandaged it up better. But there was no time to waste now.

Avery used her knowledge of the back country roads from all those years at her uncle's house to guide her to the location she'd been given.

Each turn took them deeper into the boonies, the trees thicker and the houses sparser. Her parents had to be okay. The only thing encouraging her that the prognosis was favorable was hearing their voices on the other end.

"Hold up." Seth placed his hand on top of hers. She pulled off to the side, the house partially in view. "Let me get out here, and I'll follow in on foot."

"You sure?"

"It'll give us an element of surprise. But I'll still be right here. Okay?" He swung the door open.

"Thank you." She squeezed his hand. His gesture melted her heart.

He lifted her hand to his lips and pressed a kiss.

The tires crunched along the gravel as she pulled into the drive. A barn sat behind the house and loomed tall over the one-story cabin. Which building should she check first? She stepped out of the car and closed the door quietly, trying to prevent anyone from knowing she was here until she scoped out the premise.

She walked along the outer edge of the property toward the silos. Something gripped her arm, and a prick dug into her skin before she had time to react.

"Glad to see you joined the party early," the person said and clamped down on her mouth so she couldn't scream. She tried to jerk out of their grasp, but her limbs grew weak and floppy. With a step of her foot, she stumbled forward, each movement more uncoordinated than the last. Panic threatened to well up, but she told herself to breathe. Seth was here. He wouldn't let anything happen.

"Where are my parents?" she asked, although the words sounded foreign coming from her lips, and she wasn't sure they were even audible.

"You'll see them soon enough." The person chuckled.

It took everything in her to turn around, and as she did, her legs crumpled, and her world cascaded into darkness.

Avery didn't know how much time had passed, but her head throbbed, and her legs were stiff like cardboard as she tried to move. A slow turn of her head sent a wave of nausea through her stomach, and she swallowed hard.

"She's awake, hon."

Her mom's voice filtered through her consciousness. Was she dreaming? Several minutes ticked by before she had the courage to open her eyes and turn her head. Bile rose once more, and she pulled in a deep breath to alleviate it.

She blinked a few times and focused in on her mom, who sat in the corner on a pile of hay, her hands bound behind her to a pole.

"Where's your bodyguard?" Her mom's look of disapproval and dissatisfaction filled Avery with shame.

"Taking care of things elsewhere," she sputtered.

"They were supposed to keep you safe. Not lead you into this trap," she huffed.

"We got your knitting needles, like you asked," Avery said, trying to create some peace. Her mom was just overwhelmed with the circumstances. And if they were going to make it out of here, she needed to think. Evaluate her surroundings. She'd dragged her parents into this mess with what she saw, and now their lives were at risk too.

A door slammed elsewhere, and she winced. It was only a matter of time before they came back in to check on them.

Her dad sat in the corner next to her mom but didn't say a word. He had his eyes closed; his head rested against the pole. A streak of caked blood dotted his face.

Avery noted her captor hadn't bothered to tie her to anything. Instead, her hands were bound in front of her, but her legs remained free.

"I found your papers, Dad. All the work you did on this case."

Her dad's eyes fluttered open, and he gave her a forced smile. "I wish we could have done more before we went into hiding."

"Did you know Walters was feeding information to the cartel?"

Her dad's face went slack.

"He tried to kill me, Dad."

"I didn't know. I'm so sorry." He closed his eyes.

"Do you know who Fireball is? The nickname?"

His lips thinned at the mention. "Right now, you need to pretend you know nothing. It's your greatest asset." He kept his tone low, and she had to strain to hear him. What did he know that he wasn't telling her? Everything seemed so complicated.

Her eyes assessed the open space around them to see if Seth had gotten in.

"See that loft up there?" Avery followed her dad's head nod to the steps that led to an upstairs area. "From here, it looks like there might be an exit. Go get backup."

She simply nodded. "I can try."

Avery went to stand up when the door opened, and Chelsea rushed in with Dominic on her heels.

Relief washed over her at the sight of her friend, alive and in one piece. Avery said, "I was worried sick about you. When I heard about the crash, I— Well, you're okay." The words tumbled out before she had time to consider if it was the right move to speak.

Except Chelsea stayed next to Dominic and wasn't thrown to the ground like a piece of waste. When she turned to face Dominic, she had a gun in her hand.

"What's going on?" Avery asked.

"Oh, be quiet," Chelsea spat. "You were always one to ask questions and get up in everyone's business."

This couldn't mean… Dear God, no. Someone might as well have punched her abdomen with the way the breath whooshed from her lungs. How could someone else she cared about betray her? It left a sour taste in her mouth, and anger threatened to bubble to the surface.

"What are you talking about? I helped you walk away from this life." Avery did her best to wave her hands in front of her, but the gesture caused her skin to rub against the raw area on her palm, and she bit her lip to keep from crying.

Chelsea let out a humorless laugh.

"What I had to offer her was too enticing to pass up." Dominic stepped forward.

"Where's the evidence?" Chelsea walked over to her and bent down to her level, her pupils dilated and moving rapidly. Her lethal stare wasn't like the girl Avery had once known.

"I don't have it."

Chelsea slapped her across the face. "Nonsense. You had one job."

"Let's just kill her now," Dominic said. "She clearly failed to deliver."

"No. Not until I know I'm not going to jail, because those pictures are hidden somewhere," Chelsea shrieked. "Where are they?"

"In ashes with the rest of the house," Avery said, and her parents gasped.

"I don't believe you," Chelsea said and lifted her gun. "Let's try this one more time."

Avery wanted to scream. Should she say it was in her purse in the car? It wouldn't change the outcome or their agenda. So, this was how she was going to die.

Where was Seth? Unless he bounded through that door, the hope of getting out of this alive seemed slim.

The seconds ticked by, and Avery was unsure of what to say. Chelsea turned the weapon and pointed it at her dad, her finger resting over the trigger.

"Tell me where it is, or he dies first. Then her." Chelsea swung the gun toward Avery's mom.

"No, don't do it. Please. It's in—" Avery said, but it was too late.

Chelsea fired the weapon.

Seth had let Avery get away in more ways than one, and the realization nearly brought him to his knees, but that kiss had been the promise of a conversation they'd have later when they got out of this mess.

He hoped.

Except right now, he couldn't find a way inside. He wasn't about to walk in the front entrance, and a shadow appeared by the side window.

What if Avery was dead already? He moved

back toward the tree line to stay out of view and called Grant.

"Avery's trapped inside and I can't get to her," he said, and propped his hand on his knee to catch his breath. The reality of the spoken words sent his pulse skyrocketing.

"I called backup, and I'm a few minutes out myself," Grant said.

"Good, just make sure everyone comes in with lights off."

"Understood."

"I need to find a way in to get Avery out of Antonio's clutches." His own words were like a stab wound to his heart. He'd messed up. His weakness had caused defeat. Seth ruffled his hair.

"Hey. You can't let the past define you like this."

"Don't you get it? I'm too weak. It only causes more harm than good."

"Nuh-uh." He imagined Grant shaking his head on the other end. "I know other people spat that in your face when you came back stateside. But your weakness is actually a good thing."

Seth took a step back, his brother's comment just like what Avery said.

"I mean it. Paul boasted in his weakness. And you know why?"

"Because God's power shone through best

that way." He'd memorized the verses from 2 Corinthians after church the other week.

"Exactly. It's never supposed to be about our strength or accomplishments. We'd become too prideful that way." Seth lifted his eyes back toward the barn as Grant's reminder washed over him. "It's all supposed to point to God's glory anyway."

The truth he'd easily forgotten sunk deeper into his soul and chiseled away at all the inadequacies he'd stacked up. Seth had pushed God aside, upset with the way life had turned out. When it was never about him in the first place.

"You're right, thank you," Seth said. Loki barked in the background, clearly aware of the conversation.

"Now, by God's grace, we'll find Avery before it's too late," Grant said.

Seth prayed he was right.

Static descended over the line, and Seth moved to the right. "Park behind the trees just before the driveway when you get here."

"Can you...that?" Grant's garbled voice said.

Seth lifted his phone to look at the bars. Cell signal was spotty. He repeated the directions.

"Got it." Grant confirmed. "Reinforcements...soon" was all Seth could make out.

Seth pulled his weapon from his lower back holster and checked to make sure it was loaded.

Five minutes later, tires halted on the gravel, and Seth made his way over to Grant. "That was speedy."

"There's no time for chitchat."

He was grateful Grant had the same sense of urgency to find Avery.

"Here." Grant opened his sunglass compartment to retrieve something and leaned over to give Seth a small earpiece. "It'll make things a whole lot easier."

Communication would be key to pulling this off. But he stared at the device, unable to put it in his ear. Because the moment he did, it would be difficult for him to listen to what happened on Grant's end and be alert to any danger lurking near him.

"Weakness reveals His strength." Grant patted his shoulder.

Seth closed his eyes and inserted the earpiece. *Lord, I cannot do this on my own. Cover me in Your grace and carry me in Your strength.*

"Let's do this." Seth trained his weapon low as he moved toward the barn.

"Can you hear me?" Grant asked, his voice ringing loud and clear in his ear.

"Copy that," he said.

One lone light shone by the door of the barn, while the house sat in darkness.

"I think we should split up and investigate

the barn first. Someone was in there earlier. I'll come around the north side, you take the south," Seth said softly.

"Sounds like a plan."

His eyes skimmed the area, refusing to be caught off guard. The sunset painted the sky in pastel colors, and in another half hour, it would be gone, along with another one of his senses.

Seth made his way up the steep incline at the side of the building perpendicular to the entrance. Voices filtered through a window that was cracked open.

"I hear people inside. There's a point of entrance. I'm going in," Seth said into the mic.

Grant tapped back twice to confirm.

The window glided with ease. Not seeing anything that set his alarm bells off or anyone else who might impose a threat, Seth climbed through. Hay bales covered the area, and loose straw littered the ground, which served in his favor and cushioned his footsteps. With one more glance behind him to make sure no one was ready to pounce in the corner, Seth knelt and peered around the edge of a bale. The bird's-eye view of the loft revealed Avery's parents in the corner down below, a woman holding a gun to them. Although he couldn't make out who it was from the side profile.

Avery sat several feet away from them, and

a man, who he presumed was Dominic, stood guard next to her. Her eyes traveled up to where he stood, and when she saw him, her eyes widened, while her features softened. He pressed his fingers to his lips.

Seth tapped his earpiece to alert Grant to his findings.

Avery's lips moved, but he couldn't hear anything.

The woman whipped around, a smirk on her face, and Seth sucked in a breath.

It was Chelsea. She was involved in this. He had to let Grant know.

Seth stood up and made his way back to the window. The straw pricked at his ankles and itched his skin. He shook his right foot to disperse of it, and when his foot touched the ground again, the floorboard gave way and pulled Seth down with it.

EIGHTEEN

Avery ducked forward and rolled to the side at the sound of the crash. Her head spun from the sudden movement, and her heart skipped a beat.

Grogginess still invaded her senses from whatever she'd been injected with.

God, I don't know how much more of this I can take. But You promise Your mercy shall follow me. I trust You to do that even now.

Light filtered to her pupils as she opened her eyes, examining the scene in front of her. Everything around her still seemed hazy, and it took mindful concentration to process.

"What was that?" Chelsea yelled.

Avery lifted her eyes to the last place she'd seen Seth. From her vantage point, a foot dangled from the loft ceiling. Avery turned to the left and hurled. She needed to distract them from finding Seth before he could escape.

Chelsea shrieked and stalked over to Avery.

She grabbed a fistful of Avery's hair and yanked her head back.

Another wave of nausea came.

"Enough games," Chelsea growled in her ear. "Go figure out what all that commotion is, Dom. The more guests invited to the party, the merrier," she said.

The room warmed up several degrees, yet Avery shivered. Gooseflesh speckled her skin. Something wasn't right. Now was when she needed to be on her A-game. Prepare to put her karate skills to use once more.

"Get up and show me where you're hiding the evidence." Chelsea yanked her to a standing position.

Avery let out a yelp from the pressure on her injury, and her head swam from the quick posture change. Her legs wobbled like Jell-O before she found the strength to stand firm. She could see the terror in her mom's eyes, but her dad gave her a knowing look and a brief nod. One of confidence that she would figure a way out of here.

"I need to know one thing, first," Avery said. If she stalled, maybe she could buy some precious time. Although Chelsea lifted her arm like she was ready to hit her again.

"You went into WITSEC after asking for my help. Was that all a hoax?" She slid her feet a few inches backward to create distance.

"I had a grand life with Dominic. We could travel anywhere. Money easily at our disposal. I had a minor error in my thinking when I said I wanted out." Chelsea laughed like it was the silliest thought she'd ever entertained. "Then you had to go and ruin it. All high and mighty, doing the right thing."

Avery's head hurt, and confusion still clouded her brain. "But you wanted out that night."

"I didn't want to end up like that other girl," Chelsea stated.

Right. The one Avery had seen brutally murdered because she'd messed with the wrong people.

"And the car accident on the bridge?"

"A mere tactic to keep you off the trail. But nothing seemed to scare you from staying the course to testify."

Avery stayed quiet, knowing there was no use explaining why she wouldn't stand by when illegal business was taking place. No amount of common sense would make it through her former friend's mindset.

"Let's get a move on." Chelsea waved the gun in her direction.

"One more thing," Avery piped up, her lips and mouth dry.

Chelsea let out a huff.

"Who's Fireball?"

Haughty laughter filled the area.

Dominic sauntered back in empty-handed. She almost shouted with relief but kept her lips sealed.

"She really doesn't know," Chelsea sputtered at Dominic.

"Know what?" he asked.

"Who Fireball is."

He smiled and shook his head. "You're looking at her."

Avery stared at the woman who'd once been someone she'd cared about and had wanted to help. Yet Chelsea had chosen her path, and she couldn't help but feel sorry for her. A mastermind behind something that would bring about her demise.

"There's no one out there. But they left a nice hole in the loft floor. And after we gave you clear instructions to come alone." Dominic breathed in Avery's face and tilted her chin up with his thumb.

Avery lowered her gaze, unwilling to give him the satisfaction of making eye contact.

"I can assure you, they will pay the price. All of you," he seethed.

"I want the proof. Where is it?" Chelsea asked.

"In my car," Avery said, despite the quiver coursing through her body. She'd run out of time to stall them. At least Seth escaped. She hoped

Seth had a plan to take out Chelsea and Dominic. Because she really didn't want to be self-reliant right now. She needed his help.

"Dominic, you know what to do."

The two exchanged some kind of nonverbal code, then Chelsea moved closer to Avery's parents.

"You need to let them go," Avery pleaded, but her words fell on deaf ears.

"Let's get a move on," Dominic said, the muzzle of his gun snug against Avery's back.

A whimper escaped from the crevice of her throat. She wasn't sure Chelsea was capable of killing someone, but she'd seen the destruction Dominic was willing to make, and being alone with him sent another tremor through her spine.

They stepped out into the cool of the night air, and her body shivered once more. She was cold and tired, but she had to think of an escape. Movement to her right caught her attention. *Please let it be Seth.*

They were only a few feet from her car, and the second Avery handed over those papers, she'd be dead. A few more steps, and she pretended to stumble over her feet, except she actually fell, her legs weak. The gravel scraped her knee and dug deep into her hands.

She turned to see Dominic bend down, and

Avery swung her elbow back, connecting it with his eye. He let out a cry and moved back.

"Hey!" Seth's commanding voice echoed like a melody in her ears.

Avery scrambled to her feet and went to run when a hand yanked her hair. This time, a scream rang from her lips.

"Don't try anything stupid like that again," Dominic threatened in her ear, and soon after, the butt of the gun collided with her skull. "Understood?"

A small nod was all she could muster as dark dots danced in her vision.

"I wouldn't try anything heroic, or she's dead." Dominic turned her around to face Seth, whose gaze never left hers. The torn look in his eyes nearly wrecked her as Dominic pulled her farther away from him, and they both realized he'd missed an opportunity to take the man down. With a gun pressed to her back, Seth wouldn't take a chance.

"Police will be all over this place. So I suggest reconsidering your move," Seth said and took a step forward. "You're not going to get away with this."

"Not a chance. I should have done away with her the moment she stepped on this property," Dominic said. "Keep moving."

Avery followed the orders, her body too sore

and exhausted to do anything different. A nap sounded like a good idea.

She reluctantly pulled her purse out of the car. Before she had a chance to tighten her grip, it was snatched out of her hand.

"In the car, now." Dominic shoved her to another vehicle and opened a door before slamming it shut behind her. He raced around the car and got in the driver's side.

She reached across the seat and fastened the seat belt out of habit. If she was about to die, it would be better doing it safely.

The engine roared to life, and Dominic sped out of the lot. A pop sounded, and the car began to bounce down the road. Dominic let out a few choice words and slammed the dashboard.

A few minutes later, another engine challenged the roar of the car as its headlights shone in the side mirror. An ATV gained momentum on their tail with Seth hunched over the handlebars. Dominic accelerated more, and dust kicked up in its wake, obscuring Seth.

He took a sharp turn, and Avery gripped the armrest to avoid slamming her head into the window.

Now was not the time to succumb to fear. Whatever happened, the Lord was by her side. She lacked nothing.

Even if that meant Seth didn't make it to her

before it was too late. Because right now, it grew harder to make out the ATV in the distance.

"Grant, do you copy?" Seth spoke into the earpiece, unconcerned with who might hear him at this point.

He coughed. The dust still lodged in his lungs.

The farther he diverged from the property, the more chance of them losing connection.

"I do, over." The voice came back staticky.

"I'm going after Avery. Dominic has her in a car heading south off the property."

"Copy that."

"Where are Avery's parents?" He held his breath, unsure of what response he'd get.

"Still trying to get to them. They're guarded by some woman."

"That's Chelsea. The one presumed dead. She's been part of this all along. Don't listen to her."

"You got it."

"How long till backup gets here?"

"Should be soon." His brother's voice came through faint.

"They better hurry up. I don't plan on losing Avery, but we need help."

The reply came back too soft to decipher.

Seth throttled the engine and closed in once more on the car's bumper. The trees crowded around the dirt road, and Seth had to duck to avoid a low-hanging branch as the leaves swayed in the breeze.

He glanced down at his phone to see if he'd gotten any signal yet. One small bar lit up the corner of his screen.

Suddenly, the car veered to the right and bounced down a hidden path Seth hadn't made out in the dark. He braked and spun around before following down the same road.

He sent off a text one handed to Grant with the license plate of the Lincoln in front of him as well as the tiny dot that showed his current location.

A thick branch smacked him on the cheek, and leaves brushed against his lips. He looked up from his device to see a tree trunk in the path of the ATV. With a jerk of the handle, he swerved out of the way and eased up on the gas.

He couldn't afford to lose sight of Avery now, so he pocketed the phone and shifted his eyes to what lay in front of him.

A new section of gravel appeared to diverge in the distance but still stayed in view of the current road the car traveled on. If he could just get in front of the Lincoln, he'd have a chance at cutting them off.

Seth verged down the path and kept his peripheral on the car. Bushes and trees began to obscure his view on the side as he drove, and he leaned forward in an attempt to see as panic welled in him.

Just when the path appeared to be the wrong choice, a clearing provided direct sight to the car, now a few feet behind him.

It was now or never.

Hopping over the brush, the ATV bumped along the ground before crossing perpendicular to the vehicle. Dominic hit the brakes, and the car skidded, then clipped the side of the ATV before it spun out and hit a tree.

Seth jumped off and pulled his weapon as he approached, praying Avery was unharmed. Smoke rose from inside, and Dominic didn't move. Standing off to the side, Seth pointed his gun and yanked open the door. The smell of burnt rubber invaded his nostrils from the airbag deploying.

A moan escaped the man's lips before he tumbled out of the driver's side onto the dirt. Seth pivoted to go check on Avery when Dominic went to push himself up. The moon's light glinted off a knife in his hand. He swiped at Seth's leg but missed and cut off some leaves in the process.

"Let it go, Dominic. It's over," Seth said, as he steadied the gun on him.

Sirens sounded and a cruiser pulled up, its

lights flashing. Dominic bounded to his feet and bolted around the bushes past the vehicle. Seth took off in a sprint after him and closed the distance just as Dominic stumbled and face-planted on the ground.

A tree root stuck out of the dirt, and Seth stepped over it before he grabbed Dominic's hands and tossed the knife aside. The man writhed in his grasp, but a pull of his shoulders behind his back caused him to stop.

"Over here," Seth yelled to the officers. "This man tried to kidnap the woman in the car."

With Dominic handcuffed and escorted away, Seth made his way back to the car and opened the passenger door.

Avery turned her head. "You came."

The soft-spoken words melted his heart.

She climbed out of the car and tripped in the process. Seth grabbed her arms to steady her, her skin warm to the touch.

"You're burning up."

"It's pretty chilly out here," Avery said. Her body shook as she curled into him.

He pressed his hand against her forehead.

"We need to get you to the hospital," he said as he gave her a once-over. His eyes traveled down to her hand, her fingers red and swollen. Her palm oozed puss and blistered.

"No, I'm fine. I just want to go home." Her

eyes pleaded with him, but he could see the weariness there.

"Uh-uh. Not until you get checked out by a doctor."

"I need to make sure my parents are okay first." Avery stifled a yawn.

"Let me see if I can get ahold of Grant." The call went straight to voice mail. Not good. He couldn't leave Avery alone, but he needed to check on everyone else.

An officer followed them back to the barn, and the area sounded eerily quiet.

"Do not leave my side, please." Seth wanted to tuck Avery under his arm, but it would impede his movement.

"I don't plan to—ever."

Seth stilled. "What do you mean?"

"I like you, Seth Brown. A lot."

They were seriously having this conversation now? His palms grew sweaty as if he were out under the sweltering sun with a heat advisory in effect. Except it wasn't the weather heating him up.

He leaned in and rubbed his thumb down her cheek, then pressed his lips to hers. Before she had time to melt into his embrace, Seth pulled back. "We'll talk about this after we make sure everyone's safe." He gave her a wink. She took his breath away, but he needed to focus on the task at hand. Her hair cascaded in waves down her shoulders and even in the dim light with sleepy eyes, she looked gorgeous.

"Let's hurry up then." She smiled. "I'm holding you to that."

They approached the barn, and a shiver ran down his spine because he had no idea what they were about to walk into. Although Grant's car was still here, it didn't bode well knowing he hadn't answered his call.

But this was not Iraq. He couldn't afford to let PTSD take over right now. Except he had people around him who'd help him through it. God would help him endure it. Everyone was going to be okay.

"We'll take the side entrance if you want to cover the front." Seth motioned to the officer.

"Copy that." The man nodded and headed in the opposite direction.

The door squeaked on the hinges, and Seth moved to the side to keep his back flush to the wall, gun aimed and ready. Avery kept up with his pace, which was a good thing, and her breath tickled his neck.

Silence mocked him. They moved their way through the array of hay bales, and in the center, a finger caught Seth's attention. In a rush, he reached the spot to find Grant unconscious while blood trickled down his temple. A second later, Avery gasped. Her father appeared unconscious and her mother had ropes around her wrists and duct tape over her mouth.

"Mom, Dad." Avery tore the tape off, and her mom groaned.

"What happened?" Avery crouched next to her parents.

Her mom licked her lips and swallowed. "She's gone."

"Who?" he asked.

"Chelsea escaped."

NINETEEN

Avery closed her eyes for a minute, the temptation to fall asleep beckoned. Her body yearned for rest, but she couldn't relax yet, even though her mom sat next to the hospital bed, her dad occupied the adjacent room, and Grant next to his. Because Chelsea was still at large.

Officers combed the surrounding area since last night, still searching for her. A marshal had been stationed outside Avery's door to monitor activity, but it provided little comfort.

Her body still ached, muscles sore in places she didn't even know were possible. But the antibiotic and pain meds they'd given her seemed to help take the edge off.

Turning her head to the side, Avery caught a sheen of happy tears welling in her mom's eyes.

"Seth better bring back a double chunk chocolate cookie." Avery smiled. He'd gone over to check on Grant and promised to bring back a snack from the cafeteria, which he claimed would give them the energy to stay alert.

"Oh, if he's anything like your dad, he'll bring back three and eat two of them." Her mom blinked several times and laughed.

Avery missed the laughter and bonding moments they had before they'd been forced to move away from each other and have limited communication. They hadn't signed up for the life she'd dragged them into, and the dark circles under her mom's eyes, the wrinkles etched on her face, showed proof of it.

"I'm sorry for pulling you into this mess and the hardship it's caused," Avery said.

"Oh, honey." Her mom braced her hand under her nose to keep the sniffles at bay. "I'm sorry for the way I've responded. Adding to the problem with my frustrations when you've had enough to worry about."

"It hurt, if I'm being honest," Avery whispered.

"I know. And when they shoved you outside the barn, I wasn't sure I'd ever see you again. Never get a chance to tell you I'm sorry." Her mom leaned over and gave her a side hug.

"I hope someday soon we can live a normal life."

"Me too, sweetheart. But know that no matter what life looks like, I'm going to do better at supporting you."

A rap on the door pulled Avery from the intimate conversation. "Looks like Seth's back with the cookies," she said. Avery's mouth watered in anticipation of the decadent chocolate dessert.

Except it was a nurse who entered with a clipboard and a wheelchair. The woman's brunette hair was pulled tightly into a high ballerina top bun. "I'm here to take you for X-rays, Ms. Sanford. Just to make sure nothing else is going on internally," she said with a thick New York accent. The brown-rimmed glasses on the tip of her nose made her appear librarianesque.

Selfishly, Avery wanted to deny the care until Seth got back, especially since they still needed to have a conversation about the words she uttered. She was less loopy now, but the phrase still rang true. Seth was a fighter. Regardless of his imperfections, being apart from him made her heart ache.

Her mom spoke up first as if she'd read her mind. "It's okay. I'll make sure Seth doesn't indulge in all the goodies himself. We'll be waiting here when you get back." She squeezed Avery's hand.

With her mom's help, Avery climbed into the wheelchair as the woman disconnected the IV tube and wheeled her out of the room. She nodded to the deputy, who saluted back as they turned past the nurses' station. They headed toward the elevator, and the seconds ticked by until the doors finally opened.

"This won't take long, will it? I've got a chocolate cookie waiting for me when I get back," Avery said, trying to make light of the situation.

"Not long at all," the nurse said, but something about her tone made Avery squirm.

"What kind of X-rays do I need exactly?" Avery inquired.

Her pain had subsided, and the doctor hadn't indicated concern for any broken bones.

The woman flipped through some papers. "Your abdomen and right leg."

"I'd like to speak with the doctor first." Avery twisted in the wheelchair to face the nurse.

"I wouldn't try that if I were you." The nurse peeled back her white coat to reveal a handgun. "Any wrong move, and bystanders won't know what hit them."

"Who are you?"

"A friend of Chelsea's." The arrogant tone came back.

"Where is she?"

"You'll see her soon enough." The nurse chuckled.

Avery braced her arms on the side of the wheelchair. "There's no way you're taking me anywhere." With the medicine in her system, her strength was back and she was ready for combat.

Someone would certainly see through the facade. Being wheeled out of the hospital underneath everyone's nose, never to be seen again, she couldn't possibly think that would actually happen. Avery had to believe the idea was ludicrous.

Although she'd been taken right out from under the marshal stationed at her door.

A cough erupted from Avery's lungs, and she moved her arm to cover her mouth. The hard metal of the gun wedged its way between her shoulder blades.

"I'm not playing games," the woman whispered in her ear as the elevator doors swung open and dinged, alerting them to their arrival in the main lobby.

"And neither am I," Avery said through clenched teeth.

They wheeled past the pharmacy and approached the front desk. A few feet and Chelsea would have her in the palm of her hand once more. The thought of being in her clutches coiled her stomach. And at the same time, so did knowing innocent people could be injured if she retaliated.

A woman sat at the front desk typing away,

focused on the task at hand. Avery let out another cough, this one fabricated, in hopes of getting the woman's attention, but to no avail. Pulling in a deep breath, she tried once more, this one a series of exasperated hacking that ended with a moan.

"I really don't feel good," she said. This time, the woman stopped what she was doing and turned in their direction.

"Your ride's just outside. You can rest when you get home," the nurse said through gritted teeth.

"But it's hard to breathe. Did the doctor put through the order for a nebulizer? There's a pharmacy right here."

"Do you ladies need any help?" The woman stood from her perch behind the desk and walked around. Avery held her breath, praying the nurse didn't react poorly.

"I think we're okay."

"We're just headed to the pharmacy." The nurse and Avery spoke simultaneously.

The lady eyed Avery, her forehead scrunched up.

"The pharmacy is right around the corner." The receptionist pointed.

The nurse and Avery rolled up to the pharmacy counter. "What's the name?" a man asked.

"Avery Sanford."

The moment the man went into the stacks to look for medicine that he wouldn't find, Avery leaned forward to grab a hydrogen peroxide bottle on the nearby display and jerked her arm backward.

The nurse gripped her arm before it could collide with her face.

"Let go of me," Avery said as she stood up and twisted to swing her other arm around, this one connecting with the woman's jaw. The nurse let out a scream.

The man came running around. "I couldn't find the name," he said in a huff.

Avery could feel the gun against her back as the nurse spoke. "I'm so sorry. The patient here is confused and just needs to get home to rest. The prescription was filled at another pharmacy."

Help. She mouthed the word, but the man ignored her.

"All right, then. You take care."

The woman guided her out of the pharmacy then walked down the hall, past the receptionist and out into the parking garage. The sound of engines echoed in the concrete space, but the chance of someone stopping to see if she needed assistance grew slim. People came and went, but no one paid attention, their minds focused on getting to their sick loved ones.

"Which way are we going?" Avery asked. If she talked, it might allow her to think through a solution better.

"Quit talking," the woman said. "It's right up here on the second level."

They turned the corner and climbed the ascending lanes of the garage, each parking spot occupied with a vehicle. Which provided plenty of spaces to hide. Heels clicked on the pavement as Chelsea made her way toward them.

Avery swiveled and connected with the nurse's abdomen. She let out a grunt as the breath whooshed from her lungs before falling backward on the concrete.

Avery wasted no time and sprinted down the incline. She needed to find help fast.

A gunshot reverberated through the area, and she ducked behind a car as screams from bystanders filled the air.

Seth sauntered into Avery's room, chocolate chip cookies and lemonade in hand. "I come bearing gifts." He rounded the corner. Avery's mom sat in a chair, but Avery's bed was unoccupied. "Where's Avery?" he asked and set the food on the tray table.

Before her mom had a chance to answer, a knock sounded on the door. Seth turned to see the doctor walk in, papers in hand. "I've got your discharge papers. Everything looks good. I suggest taking a few days to recoup." He looked up from the clipboard. "Is Ms. Sanford in the restroom?" he asked.

Avery's mom narrowed her eyes. "No." She drew out the word. "A nurse came to take her for X-rays. That you ordered," she said, her tone sharp.

"I'm sorry, but I think there's been some confusion. I didn't order any tests."

Seth listened, and dread formed in his stomach. "Then where is she?" he asked, but didn't wait for a response. He sprinted from the room.

"Who took Avery?" Seth loomed in front of the marshal. His face mere inches from the man.

"One of the nurses wheeled her out." He furrowed his brow.

"Don't let anyone into this room or near her parents. Got it? I'm going to find Avery."

"That's my job," the deputy stated.

There was no time to argue with the man.

"Have you seen Avery Sanford?" Seth shot off a quick description to those at the nurse's station.

"I think she was taken that way," one of the women pointed toward the elevator.

When the elevator didn't open after several attempts, Seth bounded down the steps. Where would she have gone? He swiveled around in the lobby and searched the names and signs listed on the directory.

Screams echoed through the foyer as people streamed through the automatic doors.

A woman clipped his shoulder as she moved inside. "What's happening?" he asked.

"There's a shooter over there." The lady pointed toward the second level. Her fingers shook and her eyes were wide.

"Call 911, okay?"

The woman nodded, and Seth took off out into the parking garage. His hand hovered over his gun holster.

He rounded the corner and collided into someone. Avery. He nearly shouted her name out of relief. "What's going on?" he whispered.

"Chelsea. She came…" Avery waved her hand. "She shot at me. And there's a woman involved who's dressed like a nurse." Avery rattled off the woman's description.

"Where's the hospital security?" Seth asked, turning in a circle. More people congregated right inside the foyer, where an officer flagged people to stay back.

"We can't let innocent people get hurt," Avery said. "But I'm not leaving you."

Seth's heart skipped a beat at her sincerity. He wanted her by his side for much longer than just this moment, and the truth almost spilled off his lips. But the conversation needed to wait for when they both were able to give it their full attention. "Good, because we still need to talk about that soon," he verbalized.

Heat crept into her cheeks, the rosy color against her ivory skin added to her cuteness.

"Avery, you can't hide forever," Chelsea's voice echoed against the concrete walls.

What do we do? Avery mouthed.

"Here." He guided her to a parking spot, and they crouched at the side of the vehicle. "Toss this to distract her while I get a better vantage point of where she is."

Avery flung the stone with a flick of her wrist, and it bounced several feet across the pavement. A gunshot went off, this time the bullet kicking up concrete and dust near the stone.

"Don't be such a coward," Chelsea yelled.

Seth wanted to give this woman a piece of his mind but closed his lips. Instead, he peered at the chrome tire of the adjacent truck to see her standing in the center of the lot. A nurse meandered her way toward Chelsea.

"That's the other woman who wheeled me out of the room," Avery said.

Seth stood up from his hiding place and trained his gun on Chelsea. "It's over," he shouted. "Police are right behind us."

Chelsea whipped around, her hair flying behind her, and she lifted her weapon. Her hand squeezed the trigger, and Seth ducked. The bullet whizzed past and hit the concrete wall. Seth took aim and fired back. The other woman sprinted down the garage's incline.

"Stop!" Avery yelled. "Don't let her get away."

Cops sprinted past Seth and tackled the woman to the ground.

Seth dropped his weapon and kept his hands visible as officers swarmed the area.

"I need medical personnel stat." He pointed toward Chelsea still sprawled on the pavement.

Paramedics dashed over to tend to her.

Avery closed the distance between them and wrapped her arms around his shoulders as sobs wracked her body.

"You're safe now." He rubbed her back and tucked his hand against the nape of her neck.

Once Seth and Avery gave their statements, he took her hand in his and escorted her to the lobby entrance.

"Are you okay?" Seth braced his hands on her arms and looked for any sign of new injuries.

"It's over." Her words rushed out with relief. "Thank you for seeing this through."

"I'm glad. Now let's go let your parents know you're alive."

They made their way back upstairs, and Seth saw them at the nurses' station, along with the deputy who hovered behind. Their voices raised a notch, and a couple visitors stopped to assess the commotion.

"Mom, Dad, it's okay. I'm here," Avery interjected.

Their faces relaxed in her presence.

Seth stood to the side while Avery explained everything. Soon her dad came over and extended his hand. "Thank you for taking care of my daughter," he said.

Seth took his hand and shook it. "You're welcome, sir."

After Avery convinced her parents and the nurses that she was okay and people didn't need to fuss over her, Seth and Avery sat in silence in the waiting room.

Now that danger wasn't hiding in the shadows, would Avery testify in the trial and move on with her life? Start fresh with a new beginning? Maybe with him? No, he couldn't make any assumptions for her without hearing it from her lips.

"What're you thinking?" Avery crossed her legs and scooted the chair in his direction.

"Just about what happens now."

"With the trial?"

"After the trial." His heart thudded in his chest, knowing her response could change the trajectory of his path quite drastically.

She stayed quiet for a few minutes, her eyes focused on the tile floor.

He hadn't been one to consider a woman in his life long term again a few days ago. But Avery Sanford had changed that. Her grit and passion for life pushed him to view situations with gusto. And she'd pointed him closer to Jesus in the process. But it was also knowing his limitations and weaknesses that scared him.

"I want to live a normal life," she said. "But you still haven't told me what's on your mind." She raised her eyebrows.

Right. She'd called him out. Putting his heart on the line couldn't cost him more than he'd already lost over the years since his deployment. Plus, she'd already expressed her affection for him at the barn. If that desire still stood. However, they still had some business to take care of first.

"Let's make sure this case is fully closed. Then I'll tell you what I'm thinking." Seth grinned, and Avery swatted his arm.

"You're going to leave me in suspense?"

"I sure am." Seth laughed.

A few weeks later, Seth and Avery made their way to the station. The bell on the door alerted people to their presence, but everyone continued with their tasks unfazed, coffee cups in hand and phones ringing.

"Can I help you?" the secretary asked as they approached the front desk.

"We'd like to speak with Grant Brown. He's expecting us," Seth said.

"One moment." The woman picked up the phone. Her perfectly yellow manicured nails tapped each number precisely.

Minutes later, Grant escorted them over to a conference room.

"What's the news?" Avery piped up.

Seth offered Avery a seat, but she declined. Instead, they all huddled in a corner of the room.

"Your imposter nurse, Christina Vasquez, talked. Gave us a list of names. And thanks to your testimony during the trial, we were able to bust this whole operation open."

"So, what are you saying?" Avery narrowed her eyes.

"You're going to be a free woman once you follow protocol with the marshals."

Avery let out a squeal and wrapped her arms around Seth's neck. He picked her up and spun her around.

With Avery tucked in his embrace, Seth turned toward Grant. *Thank you*, he mouthed.

Once in the parking lot, Seth said, "This is certainly cause for celebration."

"What do you have in mind?" Avery asked, her features glowing with a new sun-kissed look.

"How about some ice cream?"

"I like the sound of that." She smiled.

With his cookie dough ice cream and her mint chocolate chip in hand, they found a table outside to sit at.

"You know, there's something I've been wondering about." Avery licked the edge of the cone to keep it from melting.

"What's that?" he asked.

"What's been on that mind of yours?"

He bit into the cone and let the cold cream melt in his mouth, buying him a few seconds.

"We've spent so much time together the last several weeks, a few of those days literally fighting for our lives. Well, your life." He clasped his hands around his cone and sobered. "I can't imagine saying goodbye. You've got me caught up in all your determination and zeal for life, and I can confidently say I've fallen in love with you, Avery Thompson." The roof of his mouth dried, but he'd said what he wanted her to know.

"I don't plan on leaving the area, if that's what you're worried about. You are a hero, Seth Brown. My hero." She took his hand in hers and squeezed it. "And I love you."

"Even with all my shortcomings? You know, I'm not perfect. And I've got some challenges—"

His words were cut off as Avery put her finger against his lips.

"None of us are perfect. I've had to learn not to rely on my own strength but to trust God." And she'd witnessed His goodness. How He'd shielded her and directed her steps, even through difficulties.

"You're right. In case you ever let how strong you are get to your head—" Seth nudged her elbow "—I'll make sure to point you to your need for Jesus.

Avery laughed. "I will hold you to that. And I think you should know something."

He swallowed. "What's that?"

"Your weaknesses are the best place for God to shine through."

Here she was speaking the truth he needed to hear. "You know, I might need to be reminded of that often."

"I'll make sure to tell you every day."

Every single day was quite a commitment. One that her eyes told him she was willing to make; the sparkle there lit up the area around him more than the sun that reflected off the table.

"Oh, really?" He leaned in closer but didn't wait for her response. Rather, he weaved his fingers through her hair and tipped her chin up before capturing her lips with his.

Because despite everything he'd been through and what he'd believed about himself, she saw past all of it to the man he was growing into. And that kind of freedom was liberating.

EPILOGUE

Eight months later

A fresh coat of snow had fallen on the ground last night, and Avery stared out the school window. The white powder sparkled in the afternoon sun like a field of diamonds. It might be colder than most enjoyed, but there was something magical about it all.

Like a new beginning.

Avery continued her walk down the hall and popped her head into Linda's classroom. A sweet English teacher who had become her mentor and planned to retire at the end of the year.

"Thanks again for your help with the lesson the other day. I think the students finally grasped the concept of citations at the end of their papers," Avery said.

"My pleasure. It was a good introductory lesson before they dive into the nitty-gritty details of it in my class."

"Agreed." Avery shifted the stack of papers in her arms that she'd spent the last thirty minutes photocopying for the activity tomorrow.

"Have fun with the carnation setup." Linda smiled.

"On my way there now. The kids seemed excited when the flowers were delivered earlier."

"That's great." Linda waved her off, and Avery made her way back down to her classroom.

As advisor for the Red Cross Club, they did an annual fundraiser to support their local chapter, and this year, the students had come up with the idea of selling carnations for Valentine's Day. Students and faculty had placed the orders last week and filled out cards for who they wanted the flowers delivered to with a short message. Now they needed to assemble them before deliveries started tomorrow during each period.

Time had flown by, and Avery couldn't believe over half the school year was completed. Or that she still had the privilege of working at the school. There were still days that fear tried to crawl into her mind, and she needed to remind herself she didn't need to look over her shoulder anymore.

Her heart ached over the decisions Chelsea

had made and the betrayal of someone she'd considered a good friend. But Avery couldn't change Chelsea's choices.

Fumbling to free her hands, Avery grappled for her phone in her pocket as it vibrated. It was Seth. The school had given him the permanent position as security guard, and Avery enjoyed having him nearby.

Don't forget about our plans tonight after your meeting. :)

The last few days, he'd been adamant about her not forgetting a surprise event he had planned for them tonight, and the suspense had piqued her curiosity. Except she'd been unsuccessful at finding any clues that pinpointed to what he had up his sleeve. But she had made sure to wear a cute outfit today. The burgundy dress with boots and a cardigan had been the perfect combination of comfy and chic.

"Wow, this is quite the display," Avery said as she walked back into her room and set the papers on her desk before joining the students.

Pink and red tablecloths draped over the desks and an array of balloons were taped to the whiteboard. Some snacks sat on the counter, and a few students nibbled on pretzels and chips while they waited for her to give instructions.

"We agreed it would be fun to make our own Valentine's Day party out of it," Kelly chimed in.

"Well, it's a great idea. Give me a few minutes, and I'll give you a rundown on what we're going to do. So, grab some snacks first," Avery said, then walked over to Grant who stood in the corner of the room, camera in hand.

"Thanks for your willingness to take photos."

"I'm happy to help." Grant waggled the camera.

When she'd discovered his secret talent for photography, Avery had asked if he would be willing to take some promotional photos of their time assembling the carnations for delivery. He'd agreed to the idea, and she was grateful, because those pictures would look much better on the school's website and in the yearbook than anything she attempted on her phone.

"How's work going?" It had taken him a couple of weeks to get back into the office after the attack at the barn, which left him with a nasty concussion and the need for physical therapy.

"It's been good. Although I was handed a new case that involved multiple jurisdictions, so it's going to be dicey." He shrugged his shoulders. "But hobbies like this help provide a reprieve."

"That's good to hear. Really, thank you for doing this."

"I wouldn't have passed it up." A twinkle lit up in his eye, and Avery furrowed her brow. He appeared too excited, but now wasn't the time to pester him with questions.

"All right, ladies and gentleman. All the flowers are over in these boxes, and the tags are on this table," Avery said. "You're going to take ribbon and tie the cards around the number of flowers the person ordered then put them in buckets over here, which will be filled with water so they stay fresh until tomorrow."

Several heads nodded in acknowledgment of the task at hand. "Any questions?"

Kelly raised her hand from the front of the group. "It's not a question, but we have a surprise for you before we get started."

"Oh, sure." Avery was taken aback by her comment.

She shifted her attention to the front of the room as the door opened, and Seth walked in. He sported tan khakis and a white button-down shirt, much fancier attire than his usual security guard uniform.

"Hi." She smiled. "Are you here to help with the packing party?"

"Something like that." He winked.

Avery turned to Grant. Was he in on something she didn't get the memo about? He didn't say anything. All he gave her was a shrug of his shoulders.

"Here you go," Kelly said, and handed Seth a bouquet of carnations with a note attached to it.

He thanked her then walked over to Avery and took her hand in his.

"This is for you." He handed her the flowers, and she read the handwritten note on the card that said:

Happy Valentine's Day, my love.
Yours truly,
Seth

"Thank you. This is so sweet," she said.

"I can't believe the wild ride we had when we first met. But I couldn't be more thankful, because I've gotten to journey through so much with you already. Through the highs and lows. With God's grace and your love, I've become a better man. And I can't imagine spending the rest of my life with anyone else but you. So, Avery Thompson—" Seth smiled and bent down on one knee "—will you marry me?"

Avery let out a gasp and tears formed in her eyes. The man she'd been bent on avoiding when she first learned he worked at the school had turned out to be an incredible person she didn't know had been missing from her life.

All of the memories and conversations from the past few months flooded to the forefront of her mind. She couldn't imagine spending the rest of her life with anyone else except him.

She leaned forward, cupped his face in her hands and stared into his eyes. It was the easiest yes she'd ever given. "A thousand times yes!" she exclaimed. Tingles worked their way through her body. She was going to spend a lifetime at Seth's side. Hopefully one that didn't involve running from killers.

He slid the diamond band on her finger and stood to kiss her, wrapping her in an embrace she never wanted to leave.

Students cheered and clapped, and a few of them let out whistles. The fast clicks of the camera captured the moment. She braced her hands on Seth's chest and turned to Grant.

"You weren't really here for the carnation sale." She bent her head back in laughter.

"Guilty as charged," he said.

"And we've got this under control now," Kelly piped up. "So, you and Mr. Brown can go enjoy the evening."

"But you need a teacher with you," she said, scrunching her brow.

"That's why you've got me." Linda lifted her arms in the air and did the iconic jazz hands.

Avery had been so caught up in the moment,

she hadn't even heard Linda enter the classroom. "So you were in on this plan too?"

"Your man here had it down to a science."

Seth guided Avery out to his car, and she couldn't help but stare at her hand intertwined in his. The ring streamed an array of colors in the sunlight.

"So, where are we headed to now?" she asked as he held open the car door.

"Our engagement party of course." A grin spread across his face.

"You amaze me, Seth Brown. I love you."

"And I love you."

As Avery stood there in Seth's embrace, she propped her chin on his shoulder and surveyed the parking lot where disaster had struck months prior. Yet she'd found freedom in entrusting every step to the Lord, along with the most unexpected partner to help her through it. Now here she was, ready to spend the rest of her life with him, and she couldn't imagine a better start to a new beginning.

* * * * *

*Find strength and determination in stories
of faith and love in the face of danger.*

*Look for six new releases every month,
available wherever Love Inspired Suspense
books and ebooks are sold.*

Find more great reads at LoveInspired.com.

Dear Reader,

I graded papers one day as a school librarian, and the security officer walked by on his rounds. That brief encounter sparked a what-if question, and this story quickly bloomed.

Seth learned to surrender his weaknesses and past to God. Avery wanted independence without a constant protection detail. Yet, she learned it's okay to ask for help. Life can feel a lot like that for us too. But when we admit our inadequacies, that's when we find freedom. How amazing is it that God shows His best when we're at our weakest? When we come to the end of ourselves, His power is manifested. It's a humble reminder that we're incapable of anything apart from His grace.

Thank you for reading *Silencing the Witness*. I hope you enjoyed Seth and Avery's story as much as I did writing it for my debut novel with Love Inspired.

Blessings,
Laura Conaway